WILD BIRD

Diane Zahler

WILD BIRD

ROARING BROOK PRESS

NEW YORK

Published by Roaring Brook Press
Roaring Brook Press is a division of Holtzbrinck Publishing Holdings Limited
Partnership
120 Broadway, New York, NY 10271 • mackids.com

Our books may be purchased in bulk for promotional, educational, or business
use. Please contact your local bookseller or the Macmillan Corporate and
Premium Sales Department at (800) 221-7945 ext. 5442 or by email at
MacmillanSpecialMarkets@macmillan.com.

Library of Congress Cataloging-in-Publication Data

Names: Zahler, Diane, author.
Title: Wild bird / Diane Zahler.
Description: First edition. | New York : Roaring Brook Press, 2023. |
    Audience: Ages 8–12. | Audience: Grades 7–9. | Summary: In fourteenth-
    century Norway, the plague has destroyed Rype's entire village, and as the sole
    survivor, she embarks on a sweeping adventure across Europe with the son
    of an English ship captain and a band of troubadours in search of a brighter
    future and a new home.
Identifiers: LCCN 2022029767 | ISBN 9781250833402 (hardcover) |
    ISBN 9781250833396 (ebook)
Subjects: CYAC: Orphans—Fiction. | Voyages and travels—Fiction. |
    Plague—Fiction. | Middle Ages—Fiction. | LCGFT: Historical fiction. |
    Novels.
Classification: LCC PZ7.Z246 Wi 2023 | DDC [Fic]—dc23
LC record available at https://lccn.loc.gov/2022029767

First edition, 2023
Book design by Veronica Mang
Printed in the United States of America by Lakeside Book Company,
Harrisonburg, Virginia

ISBN 978-1-250-83340-2

10 9 8 7 6 5 4 3 2 1

For Jan and Norman
Sove nå, sove nå

We see death coming into our midst like black smoke, a plague which cuts off the young, a rootless phantom which has no mercy for fair countenance.

—Ieuan Gethen, 1349

Before

Her name was Rype.

    That wasn't really her name. It was what the strangers called her. She didn't remember her real name.

    She didn't remember anything at all.

She was hiding when the boy found her, though she wasn't sure why. She only knew that she was hungry, desperately hungry, and freezing cold. She wore just a wool kirtle over her shift, no cloak or hood. The boy's eyes widened when he peered into the hollow tree trunk and saw her crouched inside. He reached in, and she pulled back as far as she could so he couldn't touch her. He didn't look cruel, but she knew there was really no way to tell. He spoke, and his words were gibberish to her. Had she forgotten language too?

The boy sat on his heels for a while outside the tree. The wind was fierce, though, and she could see him start to shiver. Soon he was trembling almost as hard as she was.

He held out a piece of something. Fish. She could smell it, because the wind was blowing into the hole in her tree. It looked like nothing, like a stick of kindling. But it was fish, she could tell. Oh, Saint Agnes, how hungry she was! He urged her with sounds and motions as if she were a dog, and she couldn't help herself. She reached out. She moved toward it.

He let her take the dried fish, and she shoved the whole stick into her mouth. It was the first food she'd eaten in . . . she didn't know. In a long time. She drooled as she chewed, and it made her ashamed. But the boy smiled. He held out another piece of fish, and she scrabbled for it, coming to the entrance of the tree hole. He spoke nonsense again. It was clear he wanted her to come out. She didn't know what to do. She was too hungry to think.

When she stumbled out of the tree, her legs stiff,

the wind hit her hard. It carried salt crystals from the sea nearby that stung her cheeks and burned her eyes. She felt almost naked outside the tree. But the boy gave her the fish and spoke in a soft voice. The sound warmed her a little.

When he turned and started down the hill to the beach, she panicked. Tree, or beach? Tree, or beach? She let out a little whimper, and the boy turned back. He motioned to her, *follow me*. So she did.

On the beach, a group of men stood together, talking. They were dressed in thick wool against the biting wind. They were much older than the boy; all of them had rough beards and lined faces. They called to the boy but fell silent when they saw her. They stared. She wanted to run, but she did not. Instead, she stopped on the sand and tucked one leg up beneath her, standing like a stork. The pose felt familiar, and comforting. It was easier to focus on balancing than to try to think. She clutched at a wooden cross that dangled from a thin leather strap around her neck.

One of the men smiled. He stepped from the others, toward her. His beard was reddish, not brown like the others. She swayed away from him, but she didn't run. The man spoke to the boy in their gibberish. Then he spoke to her, and she understood him.

"You look like wild bird—*rype*," he said. Some of his words were wrong, and the accent was strange. "Where your people are, Rype?"

The girl stared at him. Rype, was that her name? It was so strange to hear a person speak. She didn't know when she had last heard speech. She tried to talk back to him, but her voice came out in a little squeak.

The man laughed. He said something to the other men, and they laughed too. "You talk like wild bird!" he said to the girl. "Where your people are, Rype?"

The girl shook her head. Something, a terrible feeling, weighed on her. Her leg folded under her and she sank down onto the cold, damp sand. Then she raised her arm and pointed, up over the dunes. The men exchanged looks, and three of them set off in that direction.

While they waited, the boy brought a blanket over to her. She took it and wrapped it around herself. It was scratchy and smelled sour, but it was warm.

After a time, the three men came back. Their faces were grim. They spoke to the red-bearded man, casting quick glances at her. His face changed to look like theirs. Their talk seemed to go on and on. A wave of sleepiness came over her, but she fought it. Had she slept in the tree? When had she last slept?

Then Red-Beard turned to her again.

"You come with us, Rype," he said. His voice was gentle. "Your people gone. All gone. Your people dead."

She twitched a little under the blanket, but she wasn't surprised. Had she known that? How could she have forgotten such a thing? Then she stood up. The boy motioned her forward again, and she followed him.

The ship was anchored a short distance off the shore. It had a high deck on each end and a single sail. There was a little dinghy on the sand, and the boy and one of the men pushed it partway into the water. The boy climbed in. He held his hand out to her. She stared at it long enough that the boy reddened and shrugged and pulled it back. Then she clambered into the dinghy. There was a big wooden barrel in the boat, and she leaned against it. The men shoved the boat the rest of the way into the water, splashing with their thick boots, and jumped in themselves. One of them took up the oars, and in a few minutes they were at the ship.

A rope ladder hung from the side of the ship. Red-Beard held the ladder steady at the bottom while two men struggled to get the barrel up onto the ship. From the deck, other men reached over the side and helped them. They noticed her and pointed, speaking loudly.

"They say girl on ship bad," Red-Beard said to her. "Bad luck."

The boy started up the ladder, looking back to make sure she noticed how he climbed. Then he beckoned to her.

"You go," Red-Beard said. "I not fear bad luck!" He laughed, showing a gap between his front teeth.

The girl pulled the blanket around her shoulders like a shawl. The dinghy rocked, but she balanced herself easily. She reached out for the rope ladder and climbed quickly, making her way up to the deck. The wind pulled at her, cold as death off the choppy water. At the top, the boy helped her over the railing, and then she was on the ship. The men—there were eight of them now on the deck—stood back from her, glaring. Bad luck.

She looked around at the ship. The raised section at the back was squared off, with a railing around it and a wooden roof. A ladder led up to it, and behind the ladder was a door. The rest of the deck was a tangle of coiled ropes and nets. The girl stepped around the ropes, ignoring the men, and followed the boy across the deck to a hole in its center. They descended a narrow staircase into a long, dark, low-ceilinged room lined with barrels. Between the barrels were bedrolls. There was a thick stench of fish and sweat, but it was warmer down there. The girl was glad for the warmth.

She didn't mind the fish smell.

The boy spoke in his strange language, moving cargo aside until he had built her a little cave of barrels with a narrow opening. Then he looked around and quickly lifted a small blanket from one bedroll, and another from a second. He handed those to her and clasped his hands as if in prayer, holding them against one cheek. He was telling her to sleep. She nodded and spread the blankets on the wide beams of the ship's flooring in the barrel cave. The boy turned to leave, then turned back. He pointed to himself.

"Owen," he said. "Oh-wen."

She nodded again.

"Owen," he repeated, insistent.

"Oh," she murmured.

"Owen."

"Owen." Her voice sounded cracked and unnatural to her.

His eyes brightened. He pointed to her, raised his eyebrows. She said nothing.

"Mary?" he asked. "Anna? Margaret? Elizabeth?"

She shook her head. He pointed again. She shivered, pulling her shawl-blanket tight.

"Rype," she whispered finally. "Rype."

Chapter One

IT WAS SEAN WHO BROUGHT ME BACK TO myself. Sean and his death.

When I opened my eyes that first morning on the ship, I wasn't truly awake. I was there but not there. It was strange how I could move about, nod to the sailors and learn their names in their funny language, cook them a stew on the deck with the wizened vegetables they offered me, and yet not be present. I suppose I was a bit mad. But they didn't seem afraid. Mostly they were kind to me, especially Owen and Red-Beard.

Red-Beard was Owen's father, I figured out, and the master of the ship. The *Saint Nicholas*. It was wonderful that he could speak my language. Owen took me to his cabin, and he showed me a drawing of the lands around the ship and the waters it passed through. He pointed out my land and his own. I couldn't see, at first, how a shape like a long nose could be my home. There were no trees in the picture, no houses or stables, no churches. But the water was colored blue and the land green, and finally I understood that the map showed only an idea of where things were, not the things themselves.

Time passed, the ship sliding past wooded coastline, where sometimes fishermen would stare, or wave, or duck behind leafless trees to hide from us. I woke up a little more each day. The air was fresh, the sun bright, the first yellow-greens of spring showing on the shore. But the nights were terrible. The memories that hid when I was awake waited for me and overwhelmed me when I slept. Two, three times a night, I would wake trembling or damp with sweat, and have to get up and pace the deck, letting the chill night wind brush away the horror.

In the daytime I learned English from Owen and the other sailors. Hamnet and Jacob especially seemed to like teaching me new words. Sean showed me hand signals that helped when I couldn't find or remember the right words—signs for *hungry*, for *sleepy*, for *get out of the way.* He used that one a lot. Red-Beard explained that, at home, Sean had a brother who couldn't hear, and they spoke to each other with their hands. Will the tillerman showed me how he steered the ship, the veins standing out on his forehead as he strained to keep on course. I learned the ropes and their purposes quickly and made myself as useful as I could. In the evenings, the sailors who were not on night duty gathered on deck and drank hard cider and sang songs. It didn't matter that I couldn't understand the words; the looks on the sailors' faces and the sound of their laughter made their meanings clear.

One night, the nightmare that woke me gasping and sweating stayed in my mind. It was a horrific scene, twisted figures spiraling down into the ruddy light of hellfire with looks of terror on their faces. Below were strange fishlike shapes armed with swords and pitchforks, waiting to tear the fallen to pieces before throwing them into bubbling pits. As fearsome as the image was, though, there was something familiar about it, and I lay back and let myself remember for a moment. Yes, it was a mural painted on the wooden wall of the church at home, a vision of the Last Judgment. I tried to see it in my mind's eye, the part of the painting that wasn't gruesome. The upper section, where the souls of the saved rose up to join the angels in Heaven. The beautiful shaft of light that pierced the pink-tinged clouds, God calling the blessed home.

The mural was near the front of the tall, narrow church. It had a bell tower, and on Sundays and feast days the bells would ring out to call us all to mass. The bells rang, too, for weddings, and for funerals. Those last days, they rang almost ceaselessly, until their silence let those of us still living know that the bell ringer— little Ole—was dead as well.

It was the first real memory I had on the ship, and it was agonizing. I couldn't bear it. I banished it, locked it back where it belonged. When my heartbeat slowed to normal, I pulled my blanket close and climbed the steps to the deck, longing for the cool air. The stars blazed both above and below, in the sky and reflected in the calm water. The few sailors on the night watch went about their duties, but I saw one figure huddled on the starboard side, near the dinghy. I went closer. It was Sean. He too had a blanket drawn around him, but beneath it he shuddered with chills.

"Sean?" I whispered. He turned toward me, and I bit my lip so hard I tasted blood. His skin was gray-ish white in the moonlight, his eyes sunk deep in their sockets. I could see drops of sweat standing on his brow.

"Sick," he managed. His teeth chattered together so hard it seemed they might knock themselves loose.

It was suddenly hard to breathe. I knew the look in his eyes, dull with illness, hazy with fear. It was part of my memories. I longed to flee—but where could I go? As Sean reached out for me, I backed away.

"Please," he whispered. His hands were rough and calloused. They were like my father's hands.

"I get master," I said, and ran.

When Red-Beard opened his cabin door, wiping the sleep from his eyes, I spoke in my own language. "Sean is ailing," I told him.

Fear flashed across the shipmaster's face. "Ailing? Sean sick?"

"The Sickness," I said, trying to keep my voice steady. "He has the Sickness." Red-Beard made the sign of the cross when I mentioned the Sickness, and I did as well, though I knew it would do no good. The shipmaster seemed unable to move.

"We must keep him warm," I told Red-Beard. "Give him fresh water."

"We bleed him?" Red-Beard asked.

"No. That would be useless."

Red-Beard called the other men on duty to him, and together they carried Sean to the hold. The sailors sleeping below woke, and when the shipmaster spoke to them, they turned away in dread and hurried up the stairs to sleep above deck. Owen wanted to stay, but I shooed him away.

"I help Sean," I said to him. "You sleep. Come later." Owen nodded and followed the others up the stairs. I knew there would be little rest for any of them. Fear of the Sickness chased away sleep.

The sailors brought the brazier with its hot coals down to the hold and then fled, and alone in the smoky dimness I tried to nurse Sean. He vomited bloody bile, and I cleaned it up. He thrashed and moaned in delirium, calling out in English.

Days passed in this way. I left the hold only a few times each day, and each time the men gathered around me to hear how it went below. Owen brought me food and water and helped me find the words I needed.

"Will he live?" Will asked, tears in his eyes. Sean and he had signed on as sailors together, were from the same village somewhere beyond the sea, or so I gathered. I didn't want to lie, so I shrugged. But I didn't have to answer. Will knew. Everyone knew what the Sickness did.

Small black marks appeared on Sean's cheeks and

then his arms and legs, and as the light of dawn came down the stairwell one morning, I saw the black boils starting in his armpits. I tried to keep him covered and warm, but he screamed in pain when the blanket touched his swellings. I tried to get him to drink, but his flailing arm knocked the cup from my hand. I did these things without thinking; my body knew what to do. It had done the same many times before.

Finally, as Owen joined me in the hold, I gave up and simply sat near Sean, bearing witness. Eventually he quieted and lay insensible, his breathing labored. To cover the terrible rasping noise he made as he tried to get air, and to try to comfort him, I began to hum, then to sing softly. The song came from the same place as the knowledge of how to nurse the sick, from the buried place in my mind.

I sang as the shipmaster came down, gazed on his man, and went away again, and as Owen brought food that I refused. I couldn't have eaten. I sang as the light in the stairwell grew strong and then weak once more, and at last faded away. I sang as Sean's breaths came slower and slower, with longer and longer pauses between inhale and exhale, and at last ended altogether. And I could not stop singing.

"Rype," Owen said. "Stop now." He put a hand on my arm. I was in a kind of trance, and he startled me back to awareness.

"Stop," he said again. "Sean is dead."

"Dead," I repeated. Another new English word.

"I'll tell Papa," Owen said. I wrapped my arms around myself. Tears burned in my eyes. I thought of Sean's brother who could not hear. What hand signal would tell him *Your brother is dead*?

"You helped him, Rype," Owen said gently. "What were you singing?" He hummed the tune to be sure I understood.

"Song for baby sleep."

"A lullaby? For a baby?"

"Lullaby," I echoed. "Yes." I reached over and pulled Sean's blanket up over his face.

The seafoam is frozen in strange whorls along the shore. I think about swimming out into the icy water. The cold would take my breath before I could really feel it. There would be no pain. But it is a sin, I know this. It would keep me from Heaven. And I long to see my mother again, and Per.

There is a ship far out in the water, but it is coming closer. I chew on my knuckles till they bleed, and the blood freezes before it can drip onto the sand. I know that the sailors will come to shore looking for food and fresh water. They will find me. They will hurt me. I cannot bear any more pain. So I run.

There is no place to run to. I know I am too weak from cold and hunger to live much longer. All I want is warmth and quiet. All I want is my family. On the hill above the beach, there is a tree, beaten and bent by the winds. Like me, it is nearly dead. Like me, it is hollow inside. I crawl into it. I am cold at first, but after a while I don't feel the cold anymore. I don't feel anything anymore.

Chapter Two

THE SAILORS WASHED SEAN'S BODY WITH
salt water and wrapped him in his blanket. It was all
he had for a shroud. Owen nailed two small pieces of
wood together as a makeshift cross. I had blood on my
kirtle, so Red-Beard gave me a sailor's outfit to wear. It
was too big, but it was clean and warm. Then the shipmaster ordered the ship anchored so everyone could
stand together as he and Barnaby placed Sean's body
on a plank. They and two of the others raised the plank
and tilted it over the side of the ship, and the shrouded
corpse slid off and plunged down into the dark water.

Owen threw the wooden cross overboard, and it
bobbed on the waves above the spot where Sean's body

had disappeared. Red-Beard said some words that I had heard before. They were Latin. I knew their meaning: "O Lord, grant him eternal rest, and let everlasting light shine upon him."

When I looked up from the prayer, I saw Barnaby glaring at me, and I remembered what the sailors had said: *Bad luck.*

Maybe they were right.

I needed to get away, needed sleep. I pushed through the crowd of sailors, but one didn't move out of my way—the tillerman, Will. Sean's friend. He stood, swaying slightly, in front of me, and I gasped when I met his eyes. They weren't the bright blue they'd been earlier in the day but had somehow darkened and sunk into the flesh of his pallid face. His forehead dripped sweat, and his cheeks, as Sean's had been, were dotted with black. I squeezed my own eyes closed. I didn't want to see. Behind my eyelids flashed the images of my mother's face, and my sister's, almost real enough to touch. And when I opened my eyes again, Will had crumpled to the deck.

After that, the men fell one after another, quickly. Will, then Hamnet, then Andrew. At first I tended them in the hold, but in the close space, the smell soon grew so foul that Red-Beard had them carried up to the deck. The healthy sailors rigged up a wall of blankets to try to keep the sick ones warm, and the weather obliged by turning springlike. But nothing helped.

Some of them lasted longer than Sean had. Hamnet held on for over a week, and it was worse for him. His boils grew enormous, as big as apples, on his neck and thighs and in his armpits, and then they split open, and pus and blood poured out. He couldn't bear the pain of the sunlight in his eyes, moaning and sobbing until Owen draped a blanket between two ropes to make a rooflike covering over him. His suffering was terrifying to watch, and when he died, we were all glad, glad to see him out of his misery and gone to God.

Eben, Peter, Jacob. When Jacob took sick, Barnaby turned on me. They were good friends, Jacob and Barnaby, and usually worked side by side. So when Jacob wobbled on his feet and his knees buckled, Barnaby pointed to me and said something in a harsh voice. Over and over he repeated the words: "She is a witch. She is a witch!"

I put down the cloth I was using to wipe the sweat and vomit from Eben's face. I thought I knew what the word meant, but I looked at Owen for clarification.

"Devil. Satan. Kill people," he said. I nodded.

"No," I said fiercely to Barnaby. "No witch. No witch!" I knew what happened to girls accused of being witches.

But Barnaby wasn't satisfied with my denial. He advanced on me, his meaty hands clenched in fists. "Women on board ship are bad luck," he said. He pointed at me again. "*You* are bad luck. Cursed. A witch." He turned to the others. "She will kill us all. We'll die, just like Hamnet."

Owen ran to get the shipmaster, and Red-Beard came quickly, pushing Barnaby aside. I was glad for his strong, stocky bulk beside me.

"Leave her be," he commanded Barnaby. "She is helping, not hurting. Can't you see that?"

"Why doesn't she get sick, if she's not a witch?" Barnaby demanded, and Red-Beard sighed and translated the question for me, though I'd understood it. But I didn't want to answer it. It would have made no difference. Barnaby believed what he believed.

"I have to get back to Eben," I said to Red-Beard.

"Leave her be," Red-Beard repeated. He was shipmaster, so Barnaby did as he said.

Then I turned and crouched over Eben, whose

agonized writhing had quieted into the hush that signaled death was near.

Seven men were gone now. Seven funerals at sea, with no resting place for the sailors but the dark water, no markers except for Owen's handmade crosses bobbing on the waves. But no one new was sick. With nobody to nurse, I gulped down sleep as if it were spring water. I was too exhausted to dream. Red-Beard ordered the anchor drawn up, and the *Saint Nicholas* moved again, close to the coast. The forested shore slipped past day by day, leaves showing green on the branches.

I had been on board for over three weeks. I wore my wool kirtle again, the blood washed from it, though the outline of the stain remained to remind me of the lost men. I could grasp some of what the sailors said to me now, and though they laughed at me when I spoke their language, they could make out my awkward words. As I'd tended the sick men, they had talked to me, as the dying do—sometimes hours of feverish nonsense, but more often tales about their homes and their families. I listened hard and learned what I could about them, though soon enough they were dead and the knowledge did no good. I understood enough to picture the lives they had lived in their faraway land. As they spoke I imagined their mothers and wives and children, their houses and animals and neighbors, trying to use their stories to crowd out my own stories, coaxed by the men's suffering from the space in my mind where they lurked.

Except for Barnaby, the sailors seemed grateful for the way I'd taken care of their mates. I was a witness to their anguish. But now that my memories had started to return, I began to feel my own anguish. When I cooked the salted fish, I thought of my beloved grandmother who had cooked most of our meals, and how she had muffled her cries of pain as the disease consumed her body and she tried so hard not to frighten the little ones. Stitching up the sails, I could remember the tiny clothes I'd sewn for baby Per, and how he died clutching my hand and whimpering, too weak to call out. When Red-Beard ruffled Owen's hair in passing, I could almost feel my own father's rough hand as I stroked it, cold and lifeless. The ache in my heart was raw, relentless.

The nightmares began again, but I was too tired not to sleep. Owen brought his bedroll nearby, so that when I cried out he was there to comfort me. He told me stories of the voyage, his first time away from home, to distract me.

"We had to sail up a river for days to get to Novgorod," he said. "It's a wild place. The men are like bears, huge, dressed in furs. The snow is deeper than the height of two men, and the cold! I thought my nose and fingers would drop off, they were so frozen."

I knew snow, but not like that. "Tell more," I begged.

"They ride in sleighs, pulled across the snow by giant horses. But in the city, the streets are made of wood, and the people keep them clear of snow. Their churches have golden spires on top that reach all the way to Heaven. They are full of gilded paintings of saints I'd never heard of—the most beautiful things I've ever seen.

"We traded for furs and salt. They needed our wool. There are not many sheep in Novgorod. So now the ship is filled with furs and salt to take back to England."

"Ah," I said, nodding. I'd wondered what the barrels and boxes in the hold contained.

"And salt fish, of course—that's the stink."

I knew salt fish too; it's what we ate for most of the winter at home. I could soak it and boil it into a broth. Not very tasty, but filling. The sailors liked it.

They were used to eating their salt fish in tough, chewy strips as they worked, not sitting around the brazier together with soup bowls.

I lay back and tried to imagine the golden churches of Novgorod filled with golden paintings. How magnificent it must be! I could sleep now, with that image in my mind.

During the day I spent some time with Red-Beard in his cabin, puzzling over the parchment maps on his table. The shipmaster pointed out kingdoms and duchies, from Castile to Bohemia to the Kingdom of Sicily, and I tried to imagine that world. So many places, all so different!

It started to rain, and the rain kept up for days. I stayed below, since the hold was aired out now from the smells of the sick. On the third day, though, desperate for the sight of sky and sea and for the fresh breeze, I came back up and stood in the drizzle on deck, watching the trees on shore skim by. Owen worked nearby, coiling up ropes.

"What that land?" I asked him. He shook his head.

"We lost so much time with the Sickness that I'm not sure. It could be Frisia."

"Frisia." I tried the word out. I had never heard of it, hadn't noticed it on the map. "How far England?"

"Maybe a fortnight—fourteen days? If we're lucky and don't sail into a storm."

The rain fell harder, and we ducked into Red-Beard's cabin. He was not at his table but lying on his bunk, his arm across his face. Owen hurried over to him.

"Papa, what's wrong? Are you ..."

Red-Beard lowered his arm, and I flinched. His skin was pale but his cheeks were flushed, his eyes dull and sunken. "No," I whispered. "Oh, Saint Agnes, no."

"It's just a little ague," Red-Beard murmured. "Don't tell the men."

Owen looked at me frantically. "What should we do? We must help him!"

"Fresh water," I said. "A cloth for head. Quick." Owen slipped out of the cabin, and I knelt at the side of the bunk. I felt Red-Beard's forehead and drew my hand back swiftly. He was burning. The Sickness was like a fire, leaving its victims blackened and scorched. I couldn't let it consume Red-Beard. I couldn't!

Owen brought a cloth dampened with fresh rain-water, and a bowl of water for Red-Beard. We raised him so he could drink, and I was glad to see that he was alert enough to gulp the water thirstily. I bathed his face again and again, trying to cool him. But nothing

I did stopped the onslaught of the Sickness. Owen covered him when he kicked off his blankets, and we forced him to drink as the heat of fever dried him out. As day became night, the black spots appeared, and later the boils began to swell. The sailors knew, of course, and I went to the door when Colin or Hugh knocked and tried to reassure them.

Owen held his father's hand as he thrashed in pain and then became still and quiet. "Sing to him, Rype," he pleaded.

I hummed the lullaby I'd sung for Sean, then began to sing, first in Norwegian, then in English.

"My mama takes me in her arms,
Dances with me back and forth.
Dance this way with the children,
Dance this way, and the child will sleep.
Sleep now, sleep now, in Jesus's name,
Jesus keep this child safe . . ."

"Is he dying?" Owen asked, his voice shaking.

"Yes," I said. I saw Owen's tears drop onto Red-Beard's blankets. But I couldn't cry.

He died just at dawn. Owen wept as he clutched his father's hand, but when the fingers grew cold he let go and helped me wash the body. One by one the sailors filed into the little cabin, made the sign of the cross, touched their shipmaster's face or hair or shoulder to say goodbye. It was clear how they loved him. Maybe I had loved him a little too, though I had known him for such a short time, and I cursed myself for my foolishness. Everybody died; how could I have forgotten that? How stupid, to love someone—anyone—who would suffer unbearably and then die.

When Red-Beard was shrouded, the men placed him on the plank. For a moment there was an uncomfortable silence. Then Barnaby stepped forward. "I'm the mate," he said. "So now I am the master. Does anyone challenge me?"

There were too few sailors left to do all the jobs that needed to be done. Nobody would challenge Barnaby; the men were glad to have someone to give them orders. But Owen caught my eye, and his uneasy look mirrored my own.

The group stood quietly as Barnaby stumbled over the Latin words: "O Lord, grant him eternal rest, and let everlasting light shine upon him." They tilted the board, and Red-Beard's body slid into the water.

"Wait!" Owen cried. "I haven't made a cross to mark the spot!" But it was too late. The white-shrouded body was gone. Owen's face twisted with grief.

I stepped up to the ship's railing. I felt around my neck for the thin leather strap I always wore. The wooden cross that hung from it was delicately carved. Papa had made it for me as a Saint Nicholas Day gift, whittling it from a piece of linden wood during the long winter evenings. It was the only jewelry I had ever owned. Quickly I untied the strap and held it out so the men could see the cross. Then I tossed it overboard. It would float, for a time at least. It would mark Red-Beard's watery tomb.

Owen looked at me, grateful. It was dreadful enough to be buried at sea, instead of the consecrated ground of a churchyard. But not to have a marker of any kind—there was something unbearable about the idea. I was glad I had saved his father that fate.

Then Barnaby stepped forward and grabbed my wrist. His fingers dug in hard enough to hurt. I tried to pull away. "You threw away your cross, Witch," he said, his voice a low growl. "You brought us the Sickness, and now you've thrown away Our Lord, and we'll all die."

I struggled in his grip, but he held me too tightly.

"No!" I cried out. "Let me go! Let me go!" I kicked out and pulled away so hard I wrenched my shoulder. I couldn't reach the knife I used for cooking and eating that I kept in my shoe, so I raked my fingernails across his face, but he didn't let go.

"Witches float," Barnaby said, gritting his teeth as blood welled in the scratches. "You'll go overboard, and if you sink, you're not a witch." He dragged me toward the railing. The others stood confused and frightened as I flailed.

"Stop!" Owen cried. "Papa would never let you do that!"

"He's dead," Barnaby said viciously. "He's dead because of her. There was no Sickness on board until she came. We'll all die if she stays!"

"Then she'll go," Owen said swiftly. "I'll row her to shore, and we'll leave her there. She won't bother us anymore."

I gasped. I looked toward the shore, a thick line of trees that came almost down to the sandy strand. There was no town, no houses anywhere in sight. If they left me there, I would starve or be eaten by wild animals. But if they threw me overboard, the cold water, still winter-frigid, would kill me before I could swim to shore.

"You take her, then," Barnaby said. I could see that even in his fear and anger, he didn't want my death on his conscience. The men muttered, but they agreed. Barnaby held me while they brought out the dinghy and lowered it to the water. Owen climbed down the ladder and waited while Barnaby pushed me to the side of the ship. I climbed over and then slowly made my way down, my shoulder aching, feeling for each rope rung with my feet.

"Sit," Owen said, low. He wouldn't meet my eyes. I pulled tight the shawl-blanket I'd fashioned myself and sat, trembling. Owen pulled hard on the oars, and the little boat skipped across the water. When the dinghy scraped onto the sandy shore, he said, "Get out."

I clambered over the side and splashed to land, wincing as the icy water soaked through my shoes. They used to belong to Hamnet; he'd had oddly tiny feet for such a large man. Then I turned to watch Owen row back.

Only—he didn't. He dropped the oars in the dinghy and climbed out himself, shoving the empty boat back into the water. I stared at him, shocked.

"They could turn on me next," he explained. "If they wanted the ship and thought I might claim it. I never trusted that Barnaby."

I looked at the ship. It was close enough that I could see the figures of the men at the railing and hear their shouts of fury. Barnaby shook his fist, and I almost laughed as the dinghy floated away on the tide.

"Come on," Owen said, holding out a hand. His gaze was frightened and kind and sorrowful all at once. I looked down at his hand, and for a moment I could almost hear the words of my mother, my friends, my neighbors, appalled at the idea of me—an unmarried girl!—touching the hand of a boy, a stranger. Going off with him into a strange land. But everyone I knew was gone. There were no rules anymore. Nothing was the way it had been. So I drew in a deep breath, took Owen's hand, and turned with him to walk into the forest.

It doesn't take long for people to turn on one another. At first the shock is so great, so many die so quickly, that we don't have time to react. But then ... Mama says people must always have someone to blame. When Erik sees that his brother is ill, he beats him and bars him from the house. Arne dies huddled against their front door. It only gets worse after that. Husbands accuse wives, wives flee from husbands. Grandchildren refuse to bring food to grandparents. The Haugness boys accuse the Amundsens of poisoning their well. There is a fight, Brand is killed. But he already bears the marks of the Sickness. He would have died anyway.

You can almost smell the fear throughout the village, like a whiff of something decaying in the woods.

Chapter Three

THE TREES WERE THICK, AND THOUGH IT was still early in the day, the woods seemed dark. We didn't go far in. "We'll keep the sea near," Owen said. "We're sure to come to a harbor town soon, and then we can see if there's a ship bound for England." The ground underfoot was damp from the rain and slippery with fallen leaves, and my feet were freezing. But the air was warmer than it had been on the windy deck of the ship, and I could see the new green of plants as they pushed their way toward the meager sunlight that filtered through the branches. Spring had come to the land while I'd been on the water.

"They come for us?" I asked.

"How could they?" Owen said. "They have no boat." We peered through the trees. In the distance, we could see that the men had raised the sail and pulled the anchor, and the ship began to move away from the coast.

"I wish we could have taken some food," Owen said.

"And clothes for warm," I agreed. We had nothing at all but what we wore.

After an hour or so of wordless walking, I spoke. "Why you go too?"

Owen shrugged. "My father is dead," he said. "Like yours. And the rest of them may die as well. I need to get home, to my mother and sister. I didn't want to die on the sea." His voice was flat. He seemed different to me than he had on the ship.

"Ah," I said.

"And I told my father I would watch over you. He liked you."

I blinked hard, feeling the familiar surge of tears. I whispered, too quietly for Owen to hear, "I liked him."

We were silent again, our footsteps crunching through the leaves the only sound. After a time, the ground grew sandier, and the trees shrank and became bushes, and then long grasses. The grasses rippled in waves, pushed by the wind. I had never seen anything like it. It was as different from the landscape I knew as milk from mead.

"Like golden sea," I murmured, and Owen nodded.

We could see a long distance now, across a land as flat as a trencher, threaded with blue streams. My feet dried, and so did my mouth, but soon we came to a brook. We had to follow it a ways from the coast before it was salt-free enough to drink. Then we lapped up the water thirstily. I wavered when I stood again; I was very hungry and a little dizzy. We waded across the stream and went on.

At last we saw a thin curl of smoke at the horizon—a fire. I hoped it was a fire in a house, a warm house with food and blankets. But I would be content with a fire outdoors, as long as someone was cooking something over it and would share.

It was a cottage, small and compact, made of stone, for there was no wood nearby to build with. Mud had been stuck between the stones to keep the wind out. The door was wood, though, and Owen knocked sharply on it.

We heard the latch lift, and a round-faced woman with red cheeks peered out. She spoke to us in a guttural-sounding language, and Owen smiled and tried to look friendly. With gestures, he attempted to show the woman that we had come from the sea, from a ship. At first she looked concerned, and I figured out that she thought we had been shipwrecked. But Owen managed to make her understand that there had been no shipwreck, that it was just the two of us, and that we needed food and shelter.

The woman smiled and stepped into the dark cottage, motioning us in. "Lys," she said, pointing to her chest.

"Owen," Owen replied, pointing to himself, and then, "Rype."

The woman nodded. She pointed in the direction of the ocean and said, "Gerrulf." She gestured as if catching a fish with a pole, then made a fish face, accurate enough that Owen laughed. Her husband must be fishing, then.

We sat on a bench near the fire, the guests of honor, while Lys tended the iron pot that hung over the low flame. The fire smoldered, and the walls and beams were black with smoke. It looked and smelled familiar enough to me that I felt comfortable, though the cottage stood alone in a sea of grass and not in a seaside village.

"We should say we are brother and sister," Owen said to me in a low voice. "It will be easier."

"But I and you . . . we speak different," I protested.

"How will they know? They don't speak English here."

Of course; that made sense. We would both sound equally foreign to everyone.

"Why the house here? Why no village?" I could hardly imagine living so far from neighbors. Who would help Lys and Gerrulf if they needed it?

Again Owen shrugged, as if he didn't much care. His eyes were squinted, as if he were holding back tears. I decided to stay quiet and leave him to his thoughts.

As the sun set outside, the door opened and the husband, Gerrulf, came in. I immediately understood why the couple lived in such an isolated place. Gerrulf's body was twisted and shortened by the curve of his spine, a hump protruding from between his shoulder blades. In a village, he would be mocked, harassed, maybe even banished because of his condition.

But Gerrulf's face was open and friendly, and he greeted us in his funny language and held up the string of fat fish he'd caught. Lys was pleased, and she pulled out an iron pan. I tried to help; I knew I could gut a fish in a minute. But I was a guest. It was not allowed.

While Lys prepared the meal, Owen and Gerrulf carried on a sort of conversation, gesturing, speaking loudly in their different languages, drawing shapes with the poker in the ashes on the hearth. I was able to figure out that there was a village or town not too far distant, a harbor with ships. That the town was called Emden, or something like it. That we were indeed in Frisia, and that the language Lys and Gerrulf spoke was Frisian.

"Every place have a language?" I asked.

"Not every place, but many," Owen told me. "Hundreds, probably."

Hundreds of languages! It didn't seem possible. "How anyone speak to anyone?"

"They speak as we do. With our hands."

I shook my head in disbelief.

"I can speak French," Owen said. "Most people in England speak French."

"French no good here," I pointed out.

"It might help in Emden, if there is a Norman or a Breton ship there. They would speak French."

I nodded to show I understood, though it wasn't really true. French, English, Frisian, Norman, Breton—the idea of that many people, all of them speaking in their own tongues, was almost unbelievable. But then I remembered that once every few years, a ship would stop in at my village, and sometimes the men aboard would speak in an unknown language. Such a visit was an event we would talk about for months. Maybe some of those sailors had been Frisian, some Norman, some English. I'd never noticed much more than their odd clothes or the strange foods they offered us in return for a fresh fish or some bread.

Lys's supper was soon ready, and we sat on benches at a rough-hewn wooden table and ate bowls of pea pottage and chunks of fried fish, washing it down with sweet ale and mopping up the drippings with dark bread. It was the best meal I had eaten in as long as I could remember.

Afterward, Lys and Gerrulf tried to convince us to sleep on the couple's own straw mattress in the corner of the room, but Owen refused. "We'll sleep before the fire," he said firmly. There was an argument in two languages, but finally our hosts were persuaded, though they insisted that we take the best blankets.

I thought I would fall asleep right away. I was full and comfortable, and the fire still crackled cozily on the hearth. But long after I could hear Gerrulf snoring in the corner, the sound of Owen's muffled sobs kept me awake. I felt almost a physical pain each time he drew a tear-shaken breath. His anguish mirrored mine. But I couldn't help him; I knew there was no way to help. After a time, his breathing slowed and finally took on the regular rhythm of sleep. And then I could sleep, too.

A change in the light inside the cottage woke me. The shutters were closed, and the room was dim still, but along the edges of the windows I could see daylight. A moment later Lys stirred, and then she rose and came to poke the fire into life. I got up to help her. This time Lys allowed me to cut the bread. A morning meal was unusual, but we were guests.

Lys threw open the door, letting the sunlight stream in. She brought in a bowl of water from the rain barrel outside, and we all splashed our hands and faces with water. Then we sat and ate chewy bread and a lump of hard cheese. Owen tried to show our gratitude with smiles and gestures, and Lys shrugged as if to say it was no trouble. But they were very poor, and I knew that the couple's generosity meant there would be less for them.

The day was fine, and warmer than the day before. Lys and Gerrulf waved as we set off, and before long the little cottage was lost to view in the tall grass.

"Hard to live, so far from all," I said as we walked.

"So lonely," Owen said soberly. "I don't know how he manages to catch enough to keep them through the winter."

By midday we could see the wall that enclosed Emden. The town rose up from the grasses, the tower of its church visible above the stone wall. We circled the wall until we came to a gate with carved stone images along the sides. I stared at the statues, fascinated. They wore crowns, and their faces were stern. The folds of their robes were so detailed, they seemed almost like real fabric. Were the figures kings, saints, prophets?

Two guards, one tall, one short, stood at the gate holding lances. As we approached, the guards lowered and crossed their lances, barring our way.

Confused, Owen said, "Let us in!" The guards didn't move. Owen spoke again, in a language I assumed must have been French. One of the guards, the short one, seemed to understand, and he shook his head. Owen asked something, and the guard answered him haltingly.

"We cannot enter," Owen told me. "The Sickness is in the town, and they fear travelers bringing more." He and the guard spoke again. Then Owen turned back to me, his expression strained.

"The harbor is closed to ships, the guard says. And all the harbors nearby. He thinks maybe all the harbors in the North. He says there are no ships, none at all." His voice shook.

"What to do?" I asked anxiously. "How to go to England?"

Once more Owen spoke to the guard, and then said, "He says we must walk."

"Walk?" I remembered Red-Beard's map and shook my head. "But . . ."

"Yes, there is an ocean in the way." I could see the distress in Owen's face. "I must get to my mother and sister!" he said. "They have no one now but me." He repeated his words in French to the guards.

It was hard to see the guards' eyes, shaded under their helmets, but the short one at least looked sympathetic. He said something to Owen, and Owen reported, "The Sickness is less in the South now. If we go south, he thinks we can find a harbor with ships that may go to England."

The taller guard shook his lance at us and spoke in a harsh voice, but the short one reached into a leather purse and took out a coin, which he tossed to Owen.

"*Merci,*" Owen said, and the guard replied, "*Bonne chance!*"

"What he say?" I asked as we turned and trudged down the road.

"He said *good luck*. And we'll need it."

We were heading away from the sea. I looked back at it, glistening in the sunlight, the rays dancing on the white-tipped waves. I had never been more than a day's walk from the ocean in my life. Every breath I'd ever taken had been seasoned with salt. What would the air taste like tomorrow?

The road was wide enough for two wagons to pass at first, but as the day went on, it narrowed. Another road joined it from the left, and later one came in from the right, but we saw no one at all. Owen didn't speak. His face was grim. The sound of gulls shrieking overhead faded as we walked inland, and the calls of spring songbirds replaced it.

"Where we are going?" I asked Owen at last, startling him from his reverie. He rubbed his eyes.

"Do you remember Papa's map?" he said.

I nodded.

"Picture the big piece of land. At the top is Frisia, where we are now. Yes?"

I was confused, so Owen stopped walking and picked up a stick. He drew a picture in the dirt of the road, and I squinted at it. It looked a bit like the map Red-Beard had showed me. Owen pointed to Frisia, and again I nodded. And there, off to the side, was

England. It seemed so close—just across a narrow stretch of ocean.

"We'll have to walk away from the sea. I don't know how far—weeks, probably. Maybe months. We have to get to the other sea on the map, the one at the bottom."

I could hardly conceive of going so far. And from there, if the drawing in the dirt was right, it was an immense distance over water back to England.

"Cannot!" I cried. "No food, no money. We have nothing! We starve. Or thieves kill us, or bears or wolves."

"Or the Sickness, most likely," Owen said. "Or we'll freeze, or die in a fire. Or drown perhaps. Or an ox will trample us." I stared at him, and he raised an eyebrow. "Maybe a star will fall to earth and crush us," he went on. "Perhaps a hart will stab us with his antlers and run through the streets of Paris with our bodies dangling before him."

My mouth twitched. "Or . . . we are eat by hungry *røyskatt*."

"By what?"

I made a face and wiggled my nose as much like a weasel as I could manage, and Owen snorted. "Nibbled to death by rabbits? Is that the best you can do?" he said. Despite himself, he was smiling.

I frowned. "Not rabbits. More fierce."

"Oh, stoats!" he said. "But what I mean is that we needn't bother to worry overmuch. We have nothing, but we have no choice. So whatever happens happens, and we will simply do our best."

"Whatever happens happens," I repeated. I liked the sound of it. And I was glad to have made Owen smile. He sounded and looked much more like the Owen on the *Saint Nicholas*.

Evening was falling and the air beginning to chill when we came to a small village, a cluster of six cottages and their outbuildings. There was none of the noise I would have expected from such a place. No children shouting, no chickens clucking, no goodwives calling from window to window. Only the gentle *shush* of the wind through the tall grass and the sudden screech of a crow disturbed the stillness.

I hung back as Owen started toward the first cottage. "We must," he said firmly. "If there is anything to eat . . ."

I nodded and walked with him.

But others had obviously been there first. There was nothing left, nothing at all. Even the mattresses had been emptied, the straw left in piles, the cloth coverings taken. The shelves were bare; no herbs or dried vegetables or meat hung from the rafters.

There were no bodies in the first two cottages, but in the third a woman lay lifeless on the bed, two babes beside her. Perhaps they'd been twins; they looked about the same size. But their skin was sunken in, like the skin of old people; the flesh had begun to pull away from their faces. I recoiled and ran out again, and Owen was fast behind me. He pulled the cottage door shut and made sure it was latched.

"God's bones," Owen swore. I was bent over, hands on my knees, panting. A long time passed with just the sound of our ragged breathing and the harsh shriek of the crows. Then I straightened and said, "The gardens."

Owen looked doubtful. "It's too early for anything to be growing."

Wordlessly I led him to a large patch of land behind the cottages. It had been sown, that was clear. The crows rose in an agitation of wings as we approached and fluttered to sit atop the bushes nearby, glaring. There was new growth, so light a green it was almost yellow, poking from the turned ground in even lines. I gave Owen a triumphant smile, and we dug quickly, pulling up tiny pea and bean shoots, and just-planted onion and turnip pieces that hadn't yet sprouted. They were filthy and shriveled—kept over from winter to be used as seed—but edible.

"They planted early. We're lucky," Owen said, brushing the dirt off a morsel of turnip.

"Find pot and water, I cook the worts. The greens add good taste."

Owen went back to the cottage where the mother and her babies lay. It was the only one that hadn't been completely emptied, and he managed to pull out a small iron pot, emerging pale and gagging. We carried our bounty into another of the abandoned huts. Owen went out again to gather bits of brush and dry branches for a fire, while I took the pot and went in search of water, for there had to be some nearby to sustain the little hamlet. I found a fresh, clear stream trickling near the gardens, and I filled the pot.

On my way back to the cottage, I heard voices, and I ducked behind an outbuilding. Peering around the corner, I saw two men, ragged and dirty, emerging from one of the empty huts. Their expressions were angry, and I saw the telltale black marks of the Sickness on the cheeks of one of them. The other picked up a rock from the ground and threw it at the hut, hard enough to make the door buckle. They went into the house where the dead woman lay and ran out again a moment later, faces twisted with fear.

Trembling, I heard them shout what must have been curses, and then they fled along the road, the sick one stumbling unsteadily, back the way Owen and I had come.

"I saw them," Owen said when I came into the cottage with my pot of water. "I was afraid they'd notice you—they were desperate."

"And ill," I said, breathing hard. "But they do not see me. I think there be many such, starving, afraid."

"We have to be careful. We've been lucky so far." Owen kindled a fire on the hearth and then took the pot from me and positioned it over the blaze. I added the vegetables and stirred, the familiar actions calming me.

The sun set late, and our pottage was ready by the time darkness fell. It wasn't much more than hot water, but it was filling, and we lay back satisfied before the crackling fire, cushioning heads on arms. Owen taught me a few words in French—*house, road, food*. But I was tired, and these new words tangled in my head with English words.

"Tell about home," I said. I wanted to try to imagine the end of our journey.

"Well," Owen began, "our village—more of a town, really—is called Gravesend. It's a harbor on a big river, the Thames. Ships are always coming in and out, from all over the world."

"From Norway?"

"From Norway, and Brittany, and Naples. You can buy almost anything on the wharves of Gravesend, before the goods go upriver to London. Wine, spices, silk . . ."

"Silk? What is that?"

"It's a fabric. Like linen, only much softer. It feels like . . . oh, like the fluff of a dandelion. The softest thing you can imagine."

"They make what things of this silk?"

"Clothes. For lords and ladies, I suppose. It's very dear."

I fingered my own kirtle, patched brownish-gray wool. I had owned two, as most girls in my village did. They were too warm in summer and not warm enough in winter, and itchy, though my linen shift kept most of the robe from touching my skin. How wonderful it would be to have a kirtle of silk!

"Once," Owen went on, "I saw a unicorn horn on the wharves, on its way to the king. A sailor said it washed up on the shore."

"No," I breathed. "A unicorn horn?" When I was

little, my grandmother had told me stories about uni-corns and other magical beasts—the griffon, the bas-ilisk, the pard.

"It was as long as a man's leg, and white as the first snow." In my mind, the horn shone with a light all its own.

"Your home?" I asked then. "It is big?"

"'Tis a wooden house. Dark-beamed, two stories high. A hall and a scullery, and upstairs two bedrooms."

"Like a lord!" I exclaimed. I heard Owen chuckle in the darkness.

"No, not really. We have all we need, though. Except . . . except we don't have Papa." After that, we were silent. Again, Owen wept quietly, and then we drifted into sleep.

I slept dreamlessly, exhausted by the long walk, until a sound outside the little cottage woke me when it was still dark. I didn't have to swim up through layers of nightmare but was alert instantly. I leaped to my feet, pulling the knife I had taken from the *Saint Nicholas* from my shoe. My heart was hammering.

"What?" Owen asked sleepily.

"Shh!" I hissed. "Something outside." We listened.

"An animal," Owen guessed. But the footfalls were

many and sounded heavy. Were there bears in Frisia? Or had the starving men come back? Owen rose, pulling out his own short knife.

There was a cough on the other side of the wall. A human cough. A rumble of voices. A sudden shout that was obviously a warning.

And then the cottage door flew open, tearing off its leather hinges and crashing against the wall.

The door flies open, and a group of men stand there. Mama picks up Per and holds him to her breast. Her eyes are wide with fear. The men have torches, and the flickering light makes them seem even taller and more menacing. They wear hoods. We cannot tell who they are, but I think they must have come from the next town, over the mountain. Their boots, beneath their white robes, are not familiar. I know the boots of everyone in town.

"Where is your husband?" one of the men asks. His voice is hoarse, as if he'd asked the same question a thousand times that day.

"He is gone hunting," Mama says. Her hands are shaking, and Per starts to cry.

"He is dead, you mean," the man says flatly. How does he know? But everyone is dead, or dying. Or would be soon enough.

"We are looking for the witch," the man says. "If we find the witch and burn her, the Sickness will leave us."

Gudrun and I keep our eyes on our stitching. My heartbeat is so loud in my ears that I fear the walls will crack with the sound of it.

"There is no witch here," Mama says firmly. She plants her feet wide. Her tone silences the baby. The men stare at her for a long moment. I barely dare to breathe. Then they back out of the doorway and are gone.

Chapter Four

I FOUND MYSELF CROUCHED IN A CORNER before I knew how I got there. I was breathless with terror, my heartbeat throbbing in my chest. Owen was beside me, his knife at the ready. There were people in the doorway; I couldn't tell how many. More than the two I'd seen earlier. Behind them, throwing their shapes into relief, a torch flickered in someone's hand.

I held my knife so tightly that my fingers ached. The ache told me that this was not just another bad dream. Thieves, brigands, highwaymen—they would find nothing of value to steal and so would surely kill us. I would not let that happen, not to me nor to Owen. I would fight. I owed it to Owen, for rescuing me from the beach, and from the ship. I couldn't fight the Sickness, I couldn't save his father, but this I could do for him. I raised the knife, ready to strike.

The torchlight filled the little room, and I squinted in the sudden glare as three others crowded in with us. They didn't seem to be holding weapons. The man in front was very small, easily a half foot shorter than I was. He carried something slung over his shoulder; I couldn't make out what it was. Behind him, the other two were cloaked and hooded, the hoods concealing their faces.

The man in front spoke, not the guttural sound of Frisian, but the more musical language that the guard at Emden had spoken. Cautiously, Owen replied. I caught the sound of my name and his, and of Emden. The man spoke again, at length, and something he said made Owen relax and lower his knife.

"What? What?" I asked frantically. "Who they are? What they want?"

"It's all right. It's all right. They're . . . performers. Troubadours. They won't hurt you."

I had never heard the word. "Troubadours?"

"They sing. Dance. Play music."

"You are English?" the short man said. His words were accented, but I could understand them. "I know your king—the glorious Edward." He pulled the object from his shoulder and showed it to us. It was oddly shaped, narrow at the top and round at the bottom, with strings that stretched from the neck to the bottom. It was made of wood that glowed in the torchlight. "I have played my lute for your king, at his palace in Westminster."

Then one of the others stepped forward, pushing off his hood. Only it wasn't a he—it was a she. A girl. Older than me, with dark curls and darker eyes.

"My brother and I are English as well," the girl said. "In our fashion. I am a troubairitz."

"A troubairitz?" Owen repeated.

"A female troubadour," she said, smiling at Owen's dumbfounded expression. "My name is Ysabella." Then she pointed to the short one. "He is Raymond." The other one she introduced as Jacme. Jacme was dark-haired as well, and very handsome, with a square jaw and the same full lips as Ysabella. He held up a long silver tube and put it to his lips. It looked a little like the *seljefløyte*, the willow flute that our neighbor Knut had once whittled for the village children. The only noise we could ever coax from it was a honking sound, like a goose. But when Jacme blew into his, it played a single note that hung, quivering and perfect, in the air. It was like birdsong. I looked at Jacme, and he lowered the instrument and smiled at me. My fear began to lessen.

"You didn't have troubadours who passed through your village?" Owen asked me. "Jongleurs? Musicians?"

"No," I replied, my heart slowing. I straightened and slipped my knife back into my leather shoe. "No musicians."

"They're mostly French, troubadours are, but they travel. They came to Gravesend sometimes, to perform at the fair. Or for lords."

"Or for the king!" Raymond said. "I am the troubadour of Philip, Duke of Burgundy." He pulled himself up to his full height, which was not very high at all. I wasn't sure who he meant, but he looked fiercely proud, and Owen seemed impressed.

The other man, Jacme, looked longingly at the cold pot on the cold fire, and I moved cautiously away from my corner. "We have food," I said.

Raymond grinned and poked his torch into the embers of the fire. It sprang back to life, the flames licking at the pot. Jacme and Ysabella put down the packs they carried and rifled through them, pulling out some salted meat, which they added to the pot, and a loaf of hard bread. In a few minutes, the stew boiled, and the rich smell of meat filled the cottage.

The troubadours removed their cloaks—heavy, expensive-looking robes—and settled before the fire. Raymond and Jacme were dressed in bright tunics, Raymond's gold, Jacme's red, and their hose were sky blue. Ysabella wore a kirtle of the same blue, embroidered with small flowers at its hem and neck. I had never seen such vivid clothing before. My shifts and kirtles were undyed, and I had never thought to stitch decorations on them.

"Is there food in the other houses?" Raymond asked. "Shall we look?"

"Everything has been taken," Owen told him. "There are . . . bodies."

"The Sickness, it is everywhere," Raymond said somberly. "We fled Bruges before they closed the city gates. The inn on the road from Bruges was closed also, and thus we end up here. But we hear the Sickness is less in the South. We travel back to Burgundy to see if my patron still lives."

I took the pot off the flame, and we took turns ladling out mouthfuls with a wooden spoon Ysabella pulled from her belongings. Jacme handed around bread and cheese. Ysabella passed a leather flask of ale, and we drank, sitting close to the crackling fire, which Owen fed with the brush he had gathered.

"And where do you go, my friends?" Raymond asked when we had emptied the pot.

"South, as well," Owen replied. "We're trying to get back to England. There are no ships from the North."

"Nothing comes in, nothing goes out," Raymond acknowledged. "So you go to Marseille?"

"I don't know," Owen said. "Will there be ships?"

"Perhaps," Raymond said, shrugging. "It is the biggest port in the South. If any ships are going, they will go from Marseille."

"Then we go to Marseille."

I liked the sound of it. *Mar-say.* I pictured a town like my village, but with more houses close together, ships crowded in the harbor like a flock of gulls.

Raymond pulled his lute to him and strummed it softly. The sound was delicate, unlike anything I had ever heard. He began to sing.

"Upon the summit of a hill
There stood a lordly castle;
Its battlements were guarded well
By steel-clad knight and vassal.
A lovely patch of garden-ground
Extended far behind it;

A lofty wall begirt it round,
And there were men to mind it.
There spread the forest tree its gloom,
There pear and apple grew,
There flourished flowers of rich perfume,
And flowers of beauty too."

His voice was low and rich, and after the first line I closed my eyes and tried to picture the scene. I didn't understand all the words, but I could imagine the castle on the hill, surrounded by a walled garden filled with flowers ... I had never seen such a thing, but I could almost envision it.

"Is there more?" Owen asked when Raymond stopped.

Ysabella laughed. "A great deal more!" she exclaimed.

"It goes on for a hundred stanzas," Raymond said. "I sang it for the glorious King Edward. He liked it very much, though it is a bawdy story. The queen, she had to be fanned by her lady-in-waiting, she blushed so hard, but the king laughed and clapped and demanded another song."

"But if you are French, why did you sing for my

king?" Owen asked. "We have been at war for as long as I can remember!"

"Ah, but it was after the terrible battle at Crécy," Raymond said, leaning back against the wall and putting down the lute. "Our king Philip wanted to be a little friendly after losing so badly. So I was—how do you say?—an offering of peace from one king to another."

"It didn't work very well," Owen pointed out.

"I take offense!" Raymond objected. "We were at peace for at least a fortnight, and it was entirely because of my playing." There was a moment of silence, and then Raymond burst out in a laugh that reminded me of an ox's bellow, and Owen laughed too. The joke was beyond my understanding, but I liked the sound of their laughter.

Sleep took hold of me then, and I curled in a ball on the dirt floor, pulling my blanket around me. But before I dozed off, I heard Raymond say, "The road to Marseille is the road we take, as far as Dijon. We can travel together."

I woke just at dawn before the others, not sure if the nighttime visitors had been a strange dream. But they were real enough, sprawled before the fire, Raymond snoring deafeningly and Jacme and Ysabella sleeping like dark angels, their lashes long on their cheeks. I tiptoed to the door and opened it just enough to peer through. It had rained in the night. A blanket of mist rose from the soggy ground, and I sighed to think of plodding along the road, my shoes wet and thick with mud.

Then I noticed what we had missed completely in the tumult of the visitors' appearance the night before: There were three horses tied up not far from the cottage, noses to the ground, one gray, one white, and one spotted and swaybacked. They were busy chewing the new growth that poked up from the ground and budded on the bushes. The spotted one raised its head and met my eyes with its deep brown gaze. Horses! We could ride! Oh, it would make all the difference in the world.

Owen joined me at the door, and his eyes widened at the sight of the horses. The relief on his face made clear to me how worried he'd been about our journey. "We will be able to move much, much faster!" he exclaimed. "It will shorten the trip by weeks."

I nodded. He had told me, on our walk from Emden, how anxious he was about his family, with nobody to bring in money for food. "If I don't return before winter, they could starve," he'd said.

"No crop, no garden?" I asked.

"Our house is in town. They have a bit of a garden, but it doesn't give nearly enough to last the winter." He'd sounded almost frantic about it. So the horses, the idea that our journey might go that much more quickly, cheered him greatly.

The others woke then, and we all went to the stream to drink and splash our faces. We quickly packed up our belongings, tying the packs onto the horses' saddles. "The palfrey is mine, and she and the gray are strong," Raymond said. "They can each take an extra person. But the Old Man will sink to his knees if he carries even a feather's weight more than his rider."

I patted the Old Man's soft nose and looked into his dark eyes. I had not often been so close to a horse and had only ridden one once. It had been bone bruising, and frighteningly high off the ground. Still, riding would be far better than walking.

"We aim for the city of Liège," Raymond told Owen. "The prince there is a friend of my patron's. It is about a fortnight's ride, without bad weather or brigands. Perhaps there will be inns open on the way."

"We have no money for inns," Owen confessed. "Only this coin." He showed Raymond the copper that the guard at Emden had tossed him.

"That will pay for the horses' feed," Raymond said. "And perhaps we will work a little for our keep."

"Work? What would we do?" Owen asked him.

"Why, sing, of course!" he said, and grinned at my horrified expression. "No, no—*une blague*, my friend. A joke. We three shall sing for our supper, and you may benefit from our great skill."

"You are very kind," Owen said.

"We are very lucky," he replied. "We are paid well for our work, and we are still alive. So we can share our luck a little bit."

I tried to mount the white horse by myself, but my awkward efforts spooked the beast. It took Owen and Ysabella both to boost me onto the saddle. I gripped the horse tightly with my legs as Ysabella mounted gracefully in front of me.

Owen fared a bit better getting onto the palfrey, though he needed a hand up, and Raymond swung himself up easily in front of him. Jacme mounted the Old Man, and we started off. I had to hold on to Ysabella to keep from sliding off the horse. I couldn't remember the last time I had been so close to another person—one who wasn't dying.

As we passed the cottage where the dead woman

lay with her babies, I felt a stab of regret. Should we have buried them, and not left them to lie unmourned on their bed aboveground? But there were so many dead. We could not bury them all.

The first hours in the saddle passed quickly. The day was cool and overcast, but the rain had ended. My fear of falling from the horse gradually faded, and Ysabella took it on herself to teach me French. Before long I could say the words for *horse*, *road*, *water*, and *Yes, I am hungry*. We stopped briefly for a meal of bread and cheese, and though mounting was easier this time for me, sitting had become uncomfortable. Each *clop* of the hackney's hooves sent a little shock of pain through my seat and up my spine.

Raymond began to sing as the sun sank behind the clouds, and Ysabella joined in, her high, sweet voice in delicate harmony with his.

> *"The summer comes with all its flowers,*
> *And orchards rich with fruit;*
> *The birds are warbling in the bower,*
> *And why should I be mute?*
> *In summer woods and summer airs,*

Delight I ever find;
And now my heart is free from cares—
The maid I love is kind."

There were others, in French, that I couldn't understand at all, but they all seemed to be about love—
amour.

"Do you sing about love only?" I asked Raymond, and he laughed.

"Most always," he replied. "The song of the troubadour is a love song. Sometimes it is a song of valiant battle, but most often the battle is the one between lovers. It can be a sad song, when lovers are unfaithful or die, or a terrible song, when illicit lovers are discovered and punished, but always there is love. As in life, eh?"

I let my thoughts rest for a moment on Skeviga, my little village. There hadn't been much time for love there—at least not that I'd noticed. You married the person who was the right age, or single, or likely to bear children. I wasn't even sure what it meant, to love someone in that way. Perhaps my mother and father had loved each other; I didn't know. Papa was always out on his boat, fishing, Mama always in the cottage, cooking, weaving, tending to her children. I knew that people in love kissed and held each other. My sister Gudrun had told me. But our parents never kissed, rarely touched.

But then I recalled the caress of my mother's hand on my cheek when I'd been sick with a fever, the expression on her face when she nursed little Per, nuzzling his downy head as he drowsed at her breast. Surely that was a kind of love. And once, when a storm blew up while my father was far from shore, I had seen the helpless fear and longing in her eyes. Now, remembering, I wondered if maybe she *had* loved him. When he returned soaked but safe, she'd rested a hand on his shoulder and given him a look I hadn't recognized. Was that love? Was it just that I hadn't understood it? For a moment my heart ached as much as my backside.

We were riding through woods now. The long grasses and scrubby bushes had gradually grown taller, and bare tree branches, luminous green with leaves in bud, scraped against my face and caught in my braid when I wasn't quick enough to duck. We hadn't passed a single person on the road for the entire day. I was glad; Raymond told a tale of brigands in England who attacked a group of lords and ladies on an outing. They stole every piece of jewelry on the company—and there were many—and took their fur cloaks and hoods, their food, and even their shoes. And finally, the robbers tied the nobles and hung them upside down by their feet from trees.

"Did they die?" Owen asked, enthralled.

"Oh no," Raymond answered carelessly. "They were found a few hours later, still upside down, shivering, and half naked, by a servant who had come looking for them when they did not return home. The greatest harm was to their reputations!" At my apprehensive look, he added, "But those things only happen in England, you know. Here, we are far too civilized."

Owen snorted, and Raymond let out his bellowing laugh.

We passed two deserted villages, not stopping to look in the wretched cottages that, even now, were being pulled back into the forest by the encroaching fingers of greening vines. Farther on, we came upon an inn, doors and windows hammered shut to keep out thieves. But the stable had been opened by other desperate travelers, and we spent the night there around a small fire, the horses nickering and snorting at the smoky air. On that first night, we passed around bread and cheese and ale and told our stories to one another.

Raymond spoke first and longest. His tale was almost a song in itself, of a young man who grew up at the French court and became a favorite of the wife of the Duke of Burgundy because of his beautiful singing voice and his flair for romantic lyrics, who performed for royalty and nobility in kingdoms as far away as the Empire of Bulgaria and the Kingdom of Portugal. To me it seemed almost too fantastical to believe.

"When I came to England, at the court of the most splendid King Edward the Third, I saw these two." He motioned to Ysabella and Jacme. "Jacme, you explain. My English is getting tired."

Jacme took up the story. "Our father was a knight, a Frenchman. He was one of Queen Isabella's men—she was the French wife of English King Edward the Second. But she was a bad woman—perhaps you know the story?" He said this to Owen, who nodded. But I didn't, so he went on.

"Queen Isabella raised an army against her husband the king, whom she hated. Our father was the commander of her army. And the soldiers took the king and put him in prison, and there he died. So his son became King Edward the Third."

I was sure I'd misunderstood the words. A king, in prison? How could this be?

"Our father was showered with lands and gifts for his part in the uprising, and we grew up at court. But we did not care for court life—only for the music there. So we began to sing and play with the court troubadours. This made our father . . . unhappy. And so—"

"And so we ran away," Ysabella finished. "When Raymond came to play, we left with him. We have been with him ever since."

Raymond grinned. "Ysabella, she sings like a bird, and Jacme is so handsome that the ladies are quite willing to overlook my . . . my physical shortcomings when he plays his flute to accompany me." He laughed, and even I had to smile at this. "I charm the crowds with my magnificent voice and words of love, and Jacme and Ysabella sing and play, and soften hearts and loosen purse strings with their beauty.

"When the Sickness came to England, we left to return to Burgundy, but we stopped in Bruges at the court of the Count of Flanders. The count took ill and died, and we fled that place as well. And you, my friends? Where do you come from—not both from England, I think?"

Owen and I exchanged a look. "I am English, a shipmaster's son," Owen said. "My father died just three days ago, and we left the ship to journey overland. We are trying to get back to England, to my mother and my sister."

"I am sorry for your loss," Raymond said soberly.

It was my turn, but I shook my head.

"Why does this one not speak?" Raymond asked, pointing to me. "We have told our stories, and now it is your turn. You must earn your place at our table!" He gestured at the bare room around us and laughed.

"We are . . . brother and sister. Like Jacme and Ysabella," Owen said.

"Oh, I think this is not so," Raymond said. "The blond hair and that accent—she is not from England. I know how you English talk. Tell us, Golden-Hair—who are you? Whence do you hail? Why do you not speak?"

Raymond's insistent questions seemed to hammer at me. My head spun, and for a moment I was back in the tree, in the cold, alone. I wished I was standing so I could pull up one leg like a bird to soothe myself, as I had on the beach. Instead I tugged at my braid hard for comfort. My heart knocked in my chest and my breathing grew shallow. The shadows that the fire threw on the walls wavered and took on a menacing life of their own, and I sprang to my feet and backed away.

"Leave me alone!" I cried, and then in Norwegian, *"La meg være alene!"*

"Ah, the Golden-Hair has a voice!" Raymond crowed. I glared at him.

Owen stood and moved toward me, but again I said, "Leave me alone." My voice came out in a growl, like an animal. I pulled out my knife and held it up, and he backed off, hands raised.

Troubled, he went back to the others, who were staring at me in bafflement. "Rype is from Norway," he said. "Her village all died of the Sickness. Everyone. We took her on the ship, and she left with me. She will come with me to my home and be my sister there."

I sank into a crouch against the rough wood wall as Jacme's and Ysabella's confusion turned to pity. I was embarrassed and bewildered at my own actions.

Raymond's expression, which a moment before had seemed so threatening, softened with understanding. He sighed. "Alas, we all have our tales of dread and horror. Anyone still alive does. Jacme and Ysabella are orphans now as well; I have lost my sister and nieces and nephew. Ah, I have seen . . ." His voice trailed off. I was glad. I didn't want to hear more tales of the Sickness.

When the others had fallen asleep, Owen came

over to me as I sat alone, trembling. "Come close to the fire," he whispered. "It's all right. He didn't mean to frighten you."

"I know," I whispered back, miserable. "I am sorry. I do not know why ..."

"It's all right," Owen said again. We crept back to the fire and arranged ourselves within reach of its heat. Outside a raw spring rain pelted down. The roof leaked a little, but we were warm and protected. As I rested my head on my arm and listened to Raymond's booming snores, I considered what Owen had said: *She will come with me to my home and be my sister there.* Something in those words both frightened and comforted me. I'd had a sister once, my beloved Gudrun; I'd had a brother. Per, whose downy head had smelled like strawberries, whose miniature fingers had grasped mine so tightly that it felt as if he gripped my heart. I had loved being a sister, had loved my brother more than anything. But I had lost them. Lost everyone. I couldn't bear to lose any more. And yet, to be a sister again ...

No, I couldn't think about it. I closed my eyes and slept.

Gudrun's betrothed is Mads, a fisherman like all the others. Mads is wild for my sister. He brings her meadow flowers, and she laughs at him but plucks one from the bunch and tucks it behind her ear. His eyes follow her when we go to church, or when she herds the sheep up the hillside, or when she tends the vegetable garden. He carries water from the well for her.

"Are you excited to be married?" I ask her one night, when Papa snores in the loft and we snuggle below on our straw mattress.

"Excited? It will be fine, I'm sure," Gudrun says. "I do hope Mama will make *pannekaker* for the marriage breakfast."

"But . . . do you love him?" I persist.

She bats me on the shoulder. "Go to sleep. You're bothering me, and I'm tired."

But I cannot sleep. My questions have made me wonder. Who is there for me? Will my husband come from a town beyond the mountain? Or will it be one of the Skeviga boys— Styr, with his scraggly hair and bad teeth, or Eyulf, who barely speaks but can haul in more fish than anyone else in town? Or will I be lucky and get Hakon, my friend, who is always kind and sometimes funny?

I will not be lucky. It will be none of them, of course.

Chapter Five

I HAD A NIGHTMARE THAT NIGHT, THE ONE that tormented me most often. I was in the pit of bodies in the Skeviga churchyard, scrabbling to get free, and the dead kept piling on, smothering me in a tangle of arms and legs, their terrible weight making it impossible to breathe. I smelled the reek of burned and rotted flesh and saw my friend Sigrid's lifeless eyes open and staring into mine. No matter how hard I tried, I couldn't climb out. I was the only one alive.

I woke gasping for air. I had cried out, and the others, except Raymond, were awake. "Are you all right?" Ysabella asked me in a low voice.

"Yes," I replied unsteadily. It was just a dream. Just a dream. But I didn't fall back asleep until nearly dawn.

The second day in the saddle was the worst. Every jounce of the horse hurt. Every inch of my body ached, even my teeth. I could tell that Owen wasn't faring much better; for most of the day his eyes were squinted against the pain. We had to sleep by the side of the road that night, but at least it didn't rain. And on the third day, as the soreness began to fade, the sun came out. Leaves unfurled themselves toward its warmth, and by afternoon the birches with their white papery trunks were fringed with pale green. I turned my face upward to feel the rays on my skin; the heat seemed to melt a frozen place inside me.

That day we passed two groups traveling. The first were merchants, their cloaks edged with fur, their oxen pulling carts piled high with wool. After efforts in what sounded like a dozen different languages, Raymond discovered that they were heading to Bruges for the annual wool fair there.

"But I thought Bruges had closed its gates," Owen said.

"They say the gates will open again for the fair. The merchants cannot afford to lose the business. It is a very big fair—and life must go on, yes?"

The second group we heard from a distance, and we were grateful that we did. The quiet forest was suddenly filled with the sound of rough French voices and hooves coming up behind us.

"Off the road!" Raymond ordered us. I gripped Ysabella's waist tightly as she guided our mount down a small incline and into a thick copse of trees. Raymond and Owen followed and behind us came Jacme on Old Man, the aged horse stumbling as he picked his way down the slope.

We peered through the branches, stroking the horses to quiet them, and saw a line of riders passing by. There must have been a dozen of them, covered shoulder to ankle in plate armor that glinted in the sun. They carried their helmets under their arms, and they were all enormously drunk, shouting and singing and wobbling wildly on their horses.

One of them slipped off his mount as I watched, landing with a metallic crash on the ground. For a moment I feared he would roll down the hill and end up at our feet, but a couple of the other soldiers noticed his fall and dismounted, helping him to his feet and trying to get him back onto his saddle. Up they boosted him, but he was too drunk to sling his leg over the saddle, so when they let him go, he slid back down. This happened three times before they enlisted a fourth man to stand on the other side of the horse, grab the soldier's leg as they boosted, and pull him onto the saddle. They had to tie him on with a rope.

"It's as good as a play!" Raymond whispered, his shoulders shaking with mirth. Even I had to cover my mouth to hold back my laughter. It felt so good to laugh—I hadn't laughed in as long as I could remember.

When the soldiers were well out of sight, we climbed back up onto the road. It was wide enough at this point for Raymond's horse and Ysabella's to walk side by side. "You see," Raymond said, "this is what happens when the war stops for a time. The soldiers have nothing to do, so they drink and grow fat. Then when the battle starts again, they do not fit in their armor and they have forgotten how to fight. It is no wonder the English are winning!"

"Will they win?" I asked. News of the great war between the French and English sometimes had come even to my tiny village from passing merchant ships. I knew it had been going on since I was a baby, but it had always been far removed from my life.

"Does it matter?" Raymond said with a shrug. "If the English win, a piece of France will become English, and then a little later the French will try to get it back again. The war will stop and start and stop. It will last a hundred years, or forever. Men do not know what to do when they are not at war."

I looked at Owen to see how he would take this. He shrugged as well, puffing his cheeks out in imitation of Raymond. "As long as the soldiers stay away from the shipping lanes, it doesn't matter to me."

"Then do you plan to be a merchant, my friend, and sail the seas trading?" Raymond asked.

"I don't know," Owen said. "My father's ship may be gone, and without a ship I have no trade. It took him years and years to buy it. And I'm not sure I want the seafaring life. I like to see places, but I also like my feet on the land. The sea . . ." His voice trailed off, and I knew he was imagining the way the sea had taken his father's body. Death at sea was a bad death, and many sailors died at sea.

"A farmer, then?" Raymond guessed. "Or a tradesman?"

"Can a man do something different than what his father did?" Owen asked. "My people have always been sailors and merchants. Weren't your people troubadours?"

Raymond laughed. "*Mon Dieu*, no! Troubadour is

a calling, not a business, nor even a choice. One finds a pen in one's hand and a song on one's lips, and the deed is done. My father sold pig entrails in a butcher shop in Dijon, and his father before him. We were a family of pork purveyors from the time of Emperor Charlemagne. And now I cannot touch the stuff."

"A lie!" Jacme called out. "He eats pork all the time!"

Raymond looked abashed, but his mouth twitched. "Well, in these perilous times, one must take what one can find, no?"

We passed a small hamlet, and there were people—planting the gardens, tending livestock, working in the fields. I was almost startled to see them. It was the first real sign of village life we'd come across. The villagers looked at us warily.

"Should we stop?" Owen wondered. But Raymond felt it was too early. He knew of an inn a bit farther on. I feared it would be shut up, like the last one, but when we arrived just as the sun was setting, we found it open and lively. Luckily, it appeared that the drunken soldiers had passed it by or turned onto another road.

Raymond spoke to the innkeeper, arranging for beds and a place for the horses, and we dismounted and unsaddled and brought our mounts into a small, crowded stable. Then we entered the inn, under a sign that showed three gold crowns.

I had never been inside an inn before. The main room was long and low and smoky from the fire in the big hearth at the far end. I could smell meat cooking. A narrow wooden table was crowded with men, and others were scattered at smaller tables along one wall. All eyes turned to us, and I shrank back. So many strangers! My heart began its familiar pounding and my mouth grew dry, but Ysabella pulled me forward to an empty table. Owen brought over stools, and we sat. In a moment a round, pretty woman with curls that matched her brown kirtle came out from what must have been the kitchen. She carried a steaming iron pot, which she placed on the long board. Immediately the crowd's attention turned from us to the food.

The woman came over to our table and spoke in what Raymond said was Dutch. "Lucky for us I know some Dutch," he said. "*Eten en drinken!* Food and drink!" he commanded the woman, and she grinned and nodded, flouncing her way back to the kitchen. Before long we had our own pot of stew and jug of ale, and we set to the business of eating.

I stuffed myself, mopping up my stew with a thick piece of brown bread and sneaking looks at the other customers. They were all men of various ages—some too young to sprout a proper beard, others too old to have hair on their heads at all. Most were prosperous looking, in well-made tunics or robes, with sturdy leather shoes on their feet. Maybe, I thought, they were all on their way to the wool fair. They too were looking—at me and at Ysabella. Their gazes made me blush and stare down at the table. It must be rare, I thought, for women to stay at inns.

After we finished the meal, Raymond stood and picked up his lute. "We will play for our supper," he announced. "And if we please well enough, perhaps for our beds as well." He and Jacme and Ysabella brought stools before the fire and sat, and as the room quieted, Raymond began to play and sing, Jacme's flute weaving a silvery thread through the melody.

> *"I travel near and travel far*
> *But never take my heart along;*
> *A lady fair has hold of it—*
> *I tell about her in my song.*
> *She sits beside a spinning wheel,*

Her hair is gold, her eyes are gray;
She waits for me most faithfully
And I'll return to her someday."

Then Ysabella sang.

"My lover's gone a-traveling
And I must wait for him alone.
I watch the road for his return,
My heart as heavy as a stone.
But others come to call on me,
A handsome boy, a gallant man—
I do not know how long to wait
Or if I will, or if I can."

I was entranced, and the crowd sat spellbound.
Then together Raymond and Ysabella sang:

"Oh, love is kind and love is cruel
And love is sweet and love is sour;
It makes a day a moment long,

It makes an instant seem an hour.
Will lovers stay or will they leave?
Can lovers ever faithful be?
The heart will fill, or it will break
Before my love comes back to me."

They sang in English, because as Raymond explained, he had written the song for "the glorious King Edward." The merchants, Owen told me in a whisper, probably knew some English as well as French; the others seemed to understand from the melancholy melody and the expressions on the singers' faces. There was a moment's quiet when they were finished, and then the room erupted in cheers and applause, the men slamming their tankards on the table in appreciation.

"They're good," Owen said to me. His eyes were fixed on Ysabella, as were the eyes of most of the others in the room. She was very beautiful, with her coil of dark hair and flashing eyes.

"They sound as angels," I replied. Owen turned his gaze to me then and smiled.

"You have such a funny way of looking at things," he said. "Everything is new for you."

I nodded. "All is new," I said. "In Skeviga—there

was nothing. No inn, no horse, no troubadour. Nothing but fish and farm."

"And do you like the new?"

I considered this question carefully. So much of what I'd seen since Owen had found me seemed beautiful— the carved gate of Emden, the waving grasses of Frisia, the inland flowers and birds that were unfamiliar to me. But there was the suffering as well, the stench of rotting bodies and the agonizing deaths on board the ship. And to see it all, I'd had to lose my family and leave my home. I had no answer. "Do you?" I asked instead.

"Yes, I do," Owen said emphatically. "When I was sailing with . . . with Papa, I loved to see the strange things we came across—dancing bears and the golden churches in Novgorod, the funny little birds with the colored beaks near Norway, the market in Stockholm . . . You've never seen such goods!" His eyes shone with excitement. "There were things I couldn't recognize at all, strange foods and animals and clothing. And the people—they are different everywhere, but the same too."

I shook my head, confused. "What you mean?"

"They look different. The people of Novgorod are thick and brown-haired, a little like bears themselves. Your people are tall, with yellow hair and blue eyes, while the Frisians seem to be more like the English. And the French, many of them, are darker."

"And how the same?"

"There are good ones, like Gerrulf and Lys, and bad ones, like those men roaming the village the other night. Greedy ones and kind ones. Gentle and rough. In every place, there are the same sorts, I think."

I liked this idea, that people were the same everywhere. I liked the way Owen saw the world. It wasn't all new to him, for he'd traveled far, but he noticed things. He thought about them.

Raymond started a French song then, a long, complicated ballad that seemed to be about a hero of ancient times. I couldn't follow it, but the tune was pretty and the crowd swayed as he and Ysabella harmonized.

Tired and sore, I dozed in my corner as Raymond, Ysabella, and Jacme serenaded the crowd. The men grew drunker and more appreciative with each tune, and then a call started up. "*Iedereen moet zingen!*" some of the men cried. "*Tout le monde doit chanter!*" shouted others.

I started awake when Owen poked me. "They say everyone must sing," he informed me. "We have to sing for our beds!"

"Oh no," I protested, rubbing my eyes. "I am no troubairitz—tell them!"

But the crowd insisted, and the innkeeper and his wife came out to join in the call. Owen stood, raising me with a hand at my elbow, and he pulled me to the front of the room. I stood behind the others, eyes cast down.

"I will sing a sailor's song," Owen said, in English and then French, "but you, Madame"—to the innkeeper's wife—"you must cover your ears." The men roared their approval. He began, in a rough voice, to sing one of the songs I had heard the sailors sing on the *Saint Nicholas*. Now I understood most of the words, and they made me blush.

"Oh, sailors on their ships alone
Are men so sad and drear,
They drown their longing for the girls
With jugs of ale and beer.
Sing hey for ships and sailors—
Sing hey for women's charms!
We sail across the seas, lads,
To lie in women's arms.

And when they land at once they go
Into the nearest inn
And there to slake their loneliness

With lustiness and sin.
Sing hey for ships and sailors—
Sing hey for women's charms!
We sail across the seas, lads,
To lie in women's arms."

By the third verse, I was red-faced but laughing, and the entire room joined in the chorus:

"In last night's port I met Marie,
A harbor of delight.
My mast stood tall and did its job
All day and half the night!
Sing hey for ships and sailors—
Sing hey for women's charms!
We sail across the seas, lads,
To lie in women's arms."

On and on Owen went, with the men slapping their thighs to the rhythm of the song and shouting out the chorus with Dutch and French and Frisian accents. It didn't seem to matter if they completely understood the words. Their meaning was as obvious as Raymond's love song.

At the end, Owen bowed deeply, and the applause was deafening. Then he gestured to me. "Now you must sing!" he told me.

I shook my head frantically. "I do not know any song!" I protested, pulling on my braid. "I cannot sing!"

"I've heard you sing," Owen reminded me. "Sing that song."

"It is a . . . a baby song. A lullaby. They are not wanting that!"

"Sing!" the men called. "*Chante! Zingen!* Sing!"

I turned anxious eyes to Raymond, who beckoned me over to him. "Sing a little of it for me," he said. "Do not worry. It is late and all are tired—time for a lullaby." His voice was calm, and I took a deep breath. As quietly as I could, I sang the first lines of the lullaby to him, and he strummed his lute gently, finding the tune. Then, standing close to Raymond, I opened my mouth and sang. I looked only at Owen, not at the crowded tables. The men gradually grew quiet in order to hear my soft voice. I sang in Norwegian in memory of my baby brother Per, for the song lived in my heart in that language. And then I sang for Owen in English, in memory of his father.

"Mamma tar meg på sitt fang,
danser med meg att og fram.
Danse så, med de små,
danse så, så skal barnet sove.
Sove nå, sove nå, i Jesu navn,
Jesus bevare barnet.

My mama takes me in her arms,
Dances with me back and forth.
Dance this way with the children,
Dance this way, and the child will sleep.
Sleep now, sleep now, in Jesus's name,
Jesus keep this child safe."

The silence was so complete when I was finished that I looked away from Owen to the long table. One of the older men, his face lined and white bearded, wiped away tears. Another bit his lip. A third patted the shoulder of his companion.

"Beautiful," Ysabella whispered.

Without warning, the inn door flew open and I jumped, my hand flying to my heart in shock. The clank of armor announced the entrance of soldiers—the drunken men who'd passed us on the road earlier, no more sober than they'd been hours before. Had they gotten lost, then, and not turned off toward another destination? They staggered through the door, all twelve of them, and in slurred French called for ale and food—and women. Ysabella reached out and gripped my hand.

"Upstairs!" Raymond ordered. "*Vite, vite!* As fast as you can!"

Ysabella yanked me away, and we raced for the narrow stairway by the kitchen door. The innkeeper's wife stood there, holding a candle and motioning us forward, and as the soldiers shouted and stumbled behind us, we followed her up the dark stairs and into a room at the top, where she slammed the heavy wooden door behind us and shoved the bolt into place.

My grandmother falls ill first. We have heard about the Sickness, but we do not know its course. It is terrible to watch. Then my uncle dies. Then my friends, and their families. The blacksmith. The miller and all his children. Papa. Nobody knows why it is happening. Have we sinned so atrociously that God cannot forgive us? Is the air befouled? Is it witchcraft? We don't gather together anymore. Each family keeps to itself. Our doors are closed to our neighbors. The littlest ones cry because they cannot play with their friends, but the rest of us know better. We must shut ourselves in to keep the Sickness out.

Chapter Six

THE JANGLE OF CLANKING ARMOR AND heavy footsteps sounded on the stairs, but then there was a sudden crash and a wild clatter and shouting that sounded profane. Though I didn't understand a word of it, I could tell that the drunken soldiers had fallen down the stairs. The innkeeper's wife snorted, and Ysabella and I started laughing.

"Idiots!" Ysabella said, giggling.

"Idiots," I agreed, and the innkeeper's wife chimed in, "*Idioten!*" We laughed so hard we had to sit on one of the two beds in the little room, holding our stomachs.

When we could stand again, the innkeeper's wife—her name was Anneke—placed the candle on a table by the bed and tiptoed to the door to listen. We could hear music and loud conversation from below. It was clear that the soldiers had been defeated by the stairs. Anneke slipped out of the room, indicating that we should bolt the door behind her, and went back to her work in the kitchen.

Wiping away tears of laughter, I pulled off my woolen kirtle and climbed into bed. The bedding smelled fresh, and the blanket was thick, though the room, far from the chimney, was cold. Ysabella folded her blue kirtle and climbed in beside me. With the heat from our bodies, the bedding quickly lost its chill.

"The soldiers will fall asleep," Ysabella said. "You don't have to fear them."

"We go before they wake, yes?"

"Yes. And they will feel too bad to bother us tomorrow."

I smiled. I'd seen my father, and most of the other men in Skeviga, the mornings after they'd had too much to drink. They walked around moaning as if their heads would topple off, stepping cautiously where usually they'd stomp, squinting against the light.

"Why you run away with Raymond?" I asked

Ysabella, raising myself on an elbow. After dozing down-stairs, I wasn't tired, and Ysabella seemed willing to talk.

"My father was a brute," Ysabella said fiercely. "In England, he was a hero, but to us he showed nothing but cruelty. We heard he died of the Sickness. I wish he had died sooner."

I hoped that the dim light hid my shocked expression. I had never heard anyone speak of a parent so harshly.

"Why he was that way?" I said. Then I wondered if I should have asked.

But Ysabella wanted to tell. "He hurt my brother, because Jacme sang. Father wanted Jacme to be a soldier, as he was himself. The king needed soldiers for the war, and it was expected that Jacme would follow Father. But Jacme, a soldier! It was absurd."

"Your father hurt Jacme?"

"Battered him—beat him. He was big—a strong man. He did not want Jacme to sing or play his flute. Every night Jacme would go out and meet with the other troubadours and perform, and every night when he returned, Father beat him. Neither of them would stop, neither would give in. It was terrible, terrible. So we ran away together."

"Poor Jacme," I said softly.

"Yes," Ysabella agreed. "He had no one to protect him. Our mother had died long before, when we were born. We are twins, you know. Born the same day."

There had been twins in Skeviga, two little girls who looked exactly alike. Edda and Elina. I remembered them running on the sand, throwing shells into the water, their yellow hair tangled, their faces always dirty. I hadn't known twins could be different sexes.

"And you stay with Raymond?" I asked.

"For a time. We owe him so much—we owe him everything. We could never have left England without him, never have made our living playing music. And he has taught us things we couldn't have learned on our own. But I want to go to Le Puy, near Avignon. I have heard that most everyone in Le Puy is a troubadour or troubairitz. It is easy to make a living there—pilgrims come through every day on their way to Spain, and they have coin to spend. We could write music all day, play music all night. It would be . . . oh, it would be marvelous!" I could see Ysabella's eyes shining in the candlelight.

"It sounds . . . marvelous," I agreed. I didn't know that word, but it sounded right for such a strange, wonderful place.

Ysabella lay back on the mattress. Her curls tickled

my cheek. "And you, Rype? Will you tell me your story?"

I was quiet. I thought of Skeviga, its wooden cottages spiraling smoke from their chimneys into the salt air, its green gardens thick with vegetables in the lingering days of summer, the nets piled in each yard waiting for the men to go out fishing. My parents and Per and Gudrun. The yellow-haired twins. My eyes filled with tears, and I pressed my lips together.

Ysabella patted my shoulder. "Perhaps another time. We should sleep. It is late." She leaned over the side of the bed and blew out the candle.

We were silent for a minute, settling into the bed, and then Ysabella said, "You have a very pretty voice."

A warmth spread through me. Nobody had ever complimented me before. I smiled to myself in the darkness. "Thank you," I whispered.

I woke once in the night to the sound of footsteps outside the door. I froze, but the steps were light, not the heavy tread of soldiers, and they moved past into the room next to ours. I could hear voices—Raymond, Owen, a few others. They were soon quiet, and I slept again.

Ysabella and I rose before dawn, dressed, and crept out of the room. It wasn't long before Raymond, Jacme, and Owen came out too, their eyes red-rimmed and shadowed from their long evening of song and drink. Behind their open door, I saw beds crowded with men, three and four to a mattress.

Raymond put a finger across his lips, and as quietly as we could, we made our way down the stairs, wincing when each old wooden step groaned under our weight. Anneke met us at the bottom, looking as bright and fresh as she had the night before. She pointed into the main room. Some of the soldiers were sprawled across the tables; others lay on the floor snoring. It was clear they wouldn't be up for some time. "*Idioten*," she whispered to us, giggling.

"*Danke*," Raymond said, handing her some coins. In return, she gave him a little bag of bread and cheese for the journey, and we slipped out the door into the faint light and fresh air of the new day.

We led the horses from the stable. I patted the long nose of my horse, which I had named Johann after my mother's brother, back in Skeviga. It walked with the same sure-footed stride as my uncle had, had the same resigned expression. I mounted without help, my soreness only an echo of what it had been.

Our talk the night before had made Ysabella chatty, and once we were on the road again, she slowed

Johann so the others couldn't hear and asked, "You and Owen—are you betrothed?"

I flushed and shook my head violently. "No!" I exclaimed. "We are . . . traveling? Traveling together. We are not together in that way."

"But—did you have a boy in your village? Before?"

I took a moment to answer. "There was someone," I said finally. "Hakon. Neighbor son, a fisherman like his father. Like all men." Hakon and I had grown up together, running through the fields and playing on the beach as children. When we grew older, he began to go out in the boat with his father, and I worked indoors and in the garden with my mother, so we saw each other less often, in church and on feast days. I had sometimes thought that we might marry, but that had seemed very far in the future. The future had been solid and sure, back then.

"Did you love him?"

"Always you talk of love!" I said. "I think you listen too much to your songs."

"But love is wonderful," Ysabella said, surprised. "Have you never been in love?"

I shook my head again. "Have you?"

Ysabella laughed. "I am almost always in love," she said. "In England, when I was only fourteen, I loved a lord's son, but he was betrothed to another. And in Bruges, I met one of the count's men. Ah, he was beautiful! He had golden hair, like yours, and green eyes."

I was intrigued. "What happened?"

"He wanted to marry me. But I would have had to stay in Bruges with him. I would never get to Le Puy. I would have been a housewife, cleaning and cooking and raising children. So I said no. And then . . . he became sick."

I knew the ending to that story. "I am sorry." We were quiet for a time. "But," I said at last, "will you not marry, then?"

"Perhaps someday I will," Ysabella said. "I think I will have to marry a troubadour, though. For how could I stop making music?"

The idea was astonishing to me. To choose one's own husband, or not to marry at all—I had never dreamed of such things. I turned them over and over in my mind.

"Perhaps I will never marry," I said. "Who would choose me? I have nothing."

"But you are beautiful," Ysabella said.

This was as startling as the idea of not marrying. I touched my long blond braid. Beautiful? Was I beautiful? What did that mean?

"And you can sing," Ysabella added. "You should become a troubairitz like me, and we can wander the world with our songs."

I laughed. "I know one song only," I pointed out. "No, two. There is a song we sing at harvest time." I hummed a little of it.

"That is pretty," Ysabella said. "You can write your own songs too."

"I cannot write."

"I can, and I shall teach you."

"You can write? Only priests can write!" Father Mathias, the priest in Skeviga, had been very proud of his ability, though it took him an hour or more to pen a line.

"My English nobleman taught me, and I taught Jacme. It helps to write down the words so we can remember."

I shook my head in wonder, and Ysabella laughed at my amazement as our horse ambled along with the others.

Days passed in this way, with riding, and nights outside by the fire or, sometimes, on a scratchy mattress in a farmhouse or a pile of hay in a stable. We had long conversations; my English and my French quickly grew better. Owen and I wore Ysabella's and

Jacme's extra cloaks, and those kept us warm as the days grew longer and the earth greened beneath our feet. Jonquils bloomed at the base of the white birches, and I inhaled the sweet scent of lilies of the valley, Saint Mary's flower. It rained often, and sometimes we had to dismount and trudge through the muck beside the horses, as their hooves grew too heavy with mud to walk with riders astride. But the rain was warmer now, and the air was a delicious mixture of smoke from cottage fires and the freshness of rainwater on growing things. I found I missed the salty ocean breezes less and less.

I studied Owen as we walked. Sometimes he looked melancholy, and I knew he was thinking of his father. Sometimes, especially when the going was slow because of mud or fallen trees, he became uneasy and frustrated, and I knew he was anxious about his mother and his little sister. He had told me her name, Alice, and described her to me. "She's small and quick, and smart," he said. "She talks constantly, and sometimes she says things that are . . ." His voice trailed off.

"What things?" I asked.

"Oh, I don't know. She has questions about everything. Always wanting to know how things work, why things are the way they are." He shook his head.

"Mama wanted her to go to a convent to be educated, but she refused. She is as stubborn as—well, no one is as stubborn as she is!"

I could picture Alice, red haired like her brother, stamping her foot at the idea of a convent. The look on Owen's face told me how much he loved her, how much he worried about her. I wished I could ease his burden, but I found it hard to talk about such things. My own burdens were so heavy, and I feared that speaking of them would make their weight even harder to bear.

I watched Jacme too, when I thought I was unobserved. He was like a dark flower himself, his body a graceful stem, his face as open and joyful as a jonquil's. He would dance sometimes, when Raymond and Ysabella played and sang beside the fire, his intricate steps and the movement of his legs and body somehow telling the story as clearly as the singers' words did. I loved to watch him dance.

"I am only a jongleur," he said regretfully to me one evening, throwing himself down beside me after a wild dance around the fire in which he acted out the parts of a lover, his beloved, and her betrayed husband, ending with the deaths of all three. "I cannot write a song for any amount of money. I have tried—"

"Oh, the worst songs you've ever heard!" Ysabella broke in, laughing.

Jacme didn't take offense. He and his sister loved to insult and tease each other. "They were quite bad, I'll admit," he said, wiping the sweat off his forehead. "I could only rhyme *love* with *above*, and *kiss* with *miss*."

"A singular lack of imagination," Raymond said fondly, reaching out to tousle Jacme's hair. "But you make up for it in other ways."

"So . . . ," I said, "a troubadour writes his own songs? And a jongleur sings the songs of others?"

"And dances," Jacme pointed out. "And plays instruments. I have more than my voice and my flute, you know. I play the tabor as well." He pulled a little drum from his bag, deerskin stretched around a circle of metal. With a few taps he had Ysabella swaying. Owen was fascinated and reached out for it, and Jacme handed it to him.

"And I can perform nearly as well on the lute as Raymond, you know," Jacme continued.

"A challenge!" Raymond cried, taking up his lute. "Here, *mon chéri,* try this one." With flying fingers, he picked an elaborate tune on the strings. Then he passed the instrument to Jacme, who copied the melody precisely, adding a flourish of his own at the end. Owen tapped out the rhythm on the tabor, picking up the skill quickly, and Ysabella and I clapped. This spurred Raymond to grab the lute back and pluck an even more complicated tune. Back and forth they went until at last, Raymond wrung his hands together and claimed he could no longer feel his fingers.

We came to a city the next day, Essen. We saw it first from a distance, its stone walls forbidding, with spires and peaks soaring above it. It was much bigger than the Frisian town where Owen and I had been refused entrance. As we drew closer, the wall seemed to rise higher and higher, and I couldn't imagine how we would ever get inside. But the gates were open, and the guards let us pass with barely a glance.

It was the first city I had ever seen. I was open-mouthed with the wild frantic bustle of it, the carts and horses parading through the mud, the tall houses whose upper stories nearly met above the narrow streets, the calls of fishmongers and coopers, drapers and poulterers. The smells were staggering, each shop letting loose its own odor: the perfume of spices and the stink of tallow, a whiff of fresh wood shavings and the foul stench of the tannery. Ysabella identified them all for me; we didn't have such smells in Skeviga. Over all the other scents was the reek of the gutters, which ran with refuse tossed from chamber pots above. I was dizzy with looking and smelling and listening.

"Do you like it?" Owen asked me. The loud noises made me flinch, but I couldn't stop staring.

"It is . . ." I had no words, even in my own language.

"Come," Raymond commanded. "We will go to the convent and find a bed for the night. I have met the abbess Katharina; she controls the city and says who may come and who must go. She does not much like me, nor my patron the duke, but she will suffer us for the sake of Christian charity."

"Is she a very good woman, then?" Jacme asked, clasping his hands together as if in prayer and gazing upward. Raymond's lips twisted.

"She is exactly as good as she must be," he said. Trying to puzzle out what he might mean, I looked at Owen, but he gave his customary shrug.

It was easy to find our way to the abbey. It was in the center of the city, attached to the cathedral, whose spire rose far taller than any other building. Overwhelmed by my own senses, I didn't notice at first the signs of the Sickness as we passed. Everyone seemed healthy, rich, full of energy. But then I began to notice houses boarded up or marked with a red *X* that Ysabella said signified illness inside. I saw a barrow filled with limp bodies, left to rot in the gutter.

The jostling of the crowd made the horses nervous, so we got off and walked, leading our mounts. I began to feel anxious, though I wasn't sure why. There was a strange feeling in the streets, a tension that found an echo in me. We passed a fish market, and the smells of fish long past their first freshness turned my stomach. And then we came out on the main square.

The square was thronged with people, circling the center area. They stood a dozen deep, so I couldn't see past them. I could hear shouting, and then a gasp went up from the assembly. Intrigued, Raymond, Jacme, and Owen tied the horses to one of the posts that ringed the square. Then they pushed through the crowd, pulling Ysabella and me with them, until we stood near enough to the front to see.

In the middle of the square was a group of men, dressed in white from waist to feet, naked from the waist up. On their heads were tall, pointed white caps, each marked with a red cross. At first I thought they carried staffs, but then I realized they were whips. Each whip had three leather tails at the end, and even from where I stood, I could see that some of the tails had sharp pieces of metal tied to them.

The men separated into groups of four. Some of them called out in a language I didn't know, and then the rest called back. Back and forth they shouted, and then they threw themselves down on the ground on their stomachs, stretching out their arms as if they were on a cross. The crowd grew silent, wondering what they would do next.

I gasped in shock as one man in each group rose, took his whip, and fiercely beat the naked backs of the other three. Then that man lay facedown, and the next in the group rose and beat the others. Blood began to flow, and the audience moaned as the sharp pieces of metal ripped the flesh of the men on the ground.

"What are they doing? Oh, what are they doing?" Ysabella cried, turning her face away. I could see her trembling as Jacme put a protective arm around her. I took shallow breaths, trying to push down the queasiness. I would have turned and run, but the crowd was so thick that I couldn't move.

"They are the flagellants," Raymond said, his voice low with horror. "I have heard of them but never seen them."

"But . . . why?" I asked. I wanted to stop watching, but somehow I couldn't. The whips rose and fell, and the crowd began to keen with each stroke of the lash.

"They think that by doing penance for their sins in this way, they will be spared the Sickness."

"And does it work?"

"Who knows? The pope has condemned them. He says they are heretics. The Church has been ordered to stop them. They are very foolish to come here, to Abbess Katharina's city."

The bands of four finished beating one another, and now all stood, swaying as their flayed backs dripped blood that soaked black into the dirt of the square. They started to sing in what Raymond said was German, their voices strong despite the pain they must have felt.

Then, from the street that led to the cathedral, a troop of mounted soldiers clattered into the square, pushing against the crowd. Their swords drawn, they advanced on the flagellants. Onlookers stumbled and fell under the feet of the horses, and people began to thrust against one another to get away. We were pushed by the throng, backward, then forward. Cries rose up as the flagellants realized that the soldiers were coming for them, and all at once everyone was screaming and shoving. Some of the horses, unnerved by the noise, bucked and spun around, and their riders sliced with their swords through the crowd. Struggling to keep on my feet, I reached for Owen's hand, but he was driven away from me by people frantic to escape.

"Rype!" he shouted, and I lunged toward the sound of his voice, but he was gone. In a moment I had lost sight of them all. I was alone in a terrified mob that seethed and surged around me as the soldiers advanced. And suddenly one of the mounted soldiers was right in front of me. He swore and pulled his steed to the right to keep from running me down. Something struck me on my forehead. An explosion of light and pain—and then, darkness.

The men go out every day that weather permits, their small dinghies dancing on the waves. It is dangerous work, fishing on those frigid waters, but they love it. They are strong, the men of Skeviga, with big bellies and hearty laughs and thick beards. My papa is the strongest of them all—he can wrestle all the others to the ground.

But one day in the spring Einar and his son Gunnar go out, and Gunnar rows them back early because Einar has collapsed. The fever has burned right through him in their hours on the sea. He seems half the size he'd been when they set off. He is strong enough to last three days, though, and Gunnar lasts four. After that, the men go fast, father and son, husband and uncle. All gone in a matter of months. Papa dies in September . . . or was it October? The winds are blowing cold by then, the ground too hard to dig graves. But we had all dug our own graves in the late summertime—big open pits, ready for winter.

Chapter Seven

I OPENED MY EYES TO DIMNESS AND SILENCE.
My head pounded like the beat of the tabor. I put a
cautious hand up and felt a huge bump on my forehead. The pain made me moan. It was worse when I
moved my head, so I stared up at the ceiling, its surface
plain and whitewashed.

A head moved into my view. A woman in a black
cowl, her face wrinkled and old, her eyes bright as a
bird's. She said something in a guttural language, and
then Ysabella's face took her place.

"You are awake!" Ysabella said, her smile broad.
"Oh, we feared you would never wake. You've been
asleep for a whole day. I've sat here and watched that

bump on your head grow and grow—like a whole new head!"

"It hurts," I whispered. Ysabella's bell-like voice sent daggers of pain through me.

"I don't doubt it," Ysabella agreed. "One of the townspeople said a soldier hit you. Lucky it was the flat of his sword! Otherwise you'd have no head at all instead of two."

Gingerly I turned my head. The room was utterly bare but for the bed I lay in and a wooden cross on the wall. There was no window, but light came in from the corridor outside the open door. The old woman—she must have been a nun—held a bowl and a cloth, and she came forward to bathe my brow. The water was cool, and though the touch of the cloth made me gasp, the coolness soothed my headache.

"Where are . . . the others?" I asked. It was hard to form words.

"They are in the men's section. This is the abbey—Essen Abbey. We are the guests of the abbess."

"I thought . . . Raymond said the abbess did not like him."

"And so she doesn't!" Ysabella said cheerfully. "But he—he interests her, it seems. And she does like our music, so we are welcome. Besides, it would not be very Christian to put us out on the street, when it was her soldier who hurt you."

Now I remembered: the flagellants and the soldiers and the wild crush of the crowd. "What did they do to them?"

"To the flagellants? They ran them out of town. The abbess says they are heretics and should be burned, but I think she would not do that. It would be impolitic, Raymond says, for many people believe they are holy, even if the pope doesn't."

"They were crazed," I said. The beating, the blood . . .

"Yes. Fear makes madmen of all of us."

That was true. I knew it well. "How did you get away?"

"The crowd pushed us along. It was very strange. My feet weren't even on the ground. It was like floating in a river, only with elbows and bad breath. When we floated by the abbey, Jacme pulled us out. We didn't realize till then that you weren't with us. Owen nearly went mad with worry."

"Did he?" I said. The idea was a little pleasing.

Ysabella smiled. "He tried to go back to the square, but it was impossible. And it wasn't long after that when the soldiers started bringing in the people who'd been crushed." Her smile faded. "Some of them were dead. There was a little boy . . ." She blinked hard. "Then they came in with you, and Jacme and I thought you were dead too. But Owen pointed out that you were breathing. Is he always so practical?"

I thought of how he had rescued me from the ship, and decided we would walk to Marseille, and had insisted on looking for food in the deserted village. "I think so," I said. "Where is he?" I had forgotten that I'd already asked. My mind felt strange and slow.

"He and Jacme and Raymond are in the men's section of the guesthouse. We are in a nunnery, after all." Ysabella's tone was light again. "The nuns put you in one of their empty cells. They wanted to look after you in the night."

I looked at the nun, who had finished sponging my face, and said, "Thank you."

The nun shrugged, and Ysabella said, "This is Sister Ottilie. She speaks only German. It is a horrible language. They all speak it here. They sound like they are always getting ready to spit."

I laughed, making my head throb. "Ysabella!" I chided, but the expression on Sister Ottilie's face hadn't changed.

"Oh, she cannot understand a single word. How can they not know French?"

"I didn't know French," I pointed out.

"Ah, but you are from Norway, out in the ocean somewhere. You couldn't help it."

I laughed again. It hurt less. I raised my head from the bed, wincing. The nun came forward, speaking rapidly, motioning to me to lie back. It sounded exactly like she was getting ready to spit.

"I think she is telling me to go away," Ysabella said as the nun made shooing gestures with her hands.

"Oh, don't," I pleaded.

"You should rest," Ysabella said firmly. "I will come back when it is dinnertime. Maybe you'll feel well enough to join us."

I closed my eyes—just for a moment—and when I opened them again, it was night.

A flickering light showed at the door, and I made out Ysabella, a candle in her hand. "Rype, are you awake?" Ysabella whispered.

"Yes," I answered. I moved my head tentatively and found the pain was much less.

"Will you come to dinner?"

The mention of eating made my mouth water. I had no idea how long it had been since I last ate.

"Yes!" I said, and sat up. Too quickly. The room spun wildly, and I closed my eyes and lay back down, but that made it worse. Now the spinning was behind my lids. Nausea rose in my throat.

"Slowly!" Ysabella said. "Take a deep breath. Again." I breathed, and the queasiness receded. "Now, roll onto your side—slow, slow." I did as I was instructed. "Swing your legs over the side of the bed, then raise yourself, just a little at a time."

It took several minutes, but I was able to sit up without fainting or vomiting. I sat at the edge of the bed while the room settled around me. Then I realized I was only wearing my shift.

"Where is my kirtle?" I asked.

"The nuns took it, and mine too. I think they are washing them. Abbess Katharina has provided us with new ones. Look!" Holding up the candle, Ysabella spun around. Her kirtle was indeed new, dark red, embroidered with gold leaves and flowers.

"Oh, beautiful!" I exclaimed.

"Here's yours," Ysabella said, pointing to a pile of folded material at the foot of my bed. I stood, a little unsteadily, and shook out the kirtle. It was the green of fir trees, and its embroidery was silver. Ysabella put the candle on the floor and helped me into the kirtle, holding it over my head as I raised my arms. The fabric was a silky, flowing, lightweight wool, falling to my ankles. The bodice had delicate tucks, shaping it to my body, and it fastened snugly around my waist, almost as if it had been made for me. It was like nothing I had ever worn, or even seen a woman wearing before.

"We are allowed to wear these? You are sure?" I asked.

Ysabella laughed. "I am sure. We won't be dining with the nuns, you know. There are some very important guests staying here, and we are to entertain them. So we must look the part. Oh, the green suits you well, Rype!"

I flushed with pleasure, then quickly rebraided my hair. "My hood . . . ," I said.

"You weren't wearing it when they brought you in," Ysabella told me. "The abbess says we may just be veiled." She held out a length of white veil, and I pinned it over my blond hair. I pushed my feet into my worn shoes. They looked even shabbier contrasted with the kirtle, but they could barely be seen under it.

"Shall we go, milady?" Ysabella said, stooping to pick up the candle and offering me her arm.

"We shall," I said, a little nervously, and took Ysabella's arm.

The corridors of the abbey were dark and quiet. I

walked slowly at first, but I soon felt stronger. Our footsteps echoed on the stones, and the candlelight showed carved angels and saints on columns and over doorways. Briefly we were outside, in a garden cloister ringed by walkways and painted columns. A sharp, sweet smell rose in the air from the plants in the center of the cloister, and the breeze nearly blew out Ysabella's candle. We passed the open door of a chapel. Inside, something glittered like a flame in the moonlight that streamed through a window. I stopped to look in.

"That is the Golden Virgin," Ysabella whispered.

I could see now that it was a statue, the Virgin Mary seated. One gilded arm wrapped protectively about the infant Jesus in her lap. The other hand was extended, as if it were beckoning. I came closer.

"She is truly gold?"

"So the abbess says. She is worth as much as the whole city."

Even in moonlight, the gold shimmered. It almost seemed as though the Virgin moved. How lovely she was! I put a hand out to touch her outstretched hand and was shocked to find it cold, as cold as death. I snatched my hand back.

"Come on," Ysabella urged. I backed out of the

chapel, and we continued down the corridor. Then we turned a corner and Ysabella pushed open a door.

The room we entered was long and high and full of light and sound. There were flickering candles everywhere. At the far end was a huge hooded fireplace with a fire roaring on the hearth. A table ran nearly the length of the room. It was set with glittering plates and goblets, and people sat all along its length. The walls were hung with tapestries, and the floor was paved with bright copper-colored tiles showing flowers and vines, birds and hunting dogs. I hardly knew where to step or where to look.

"Rype!" Owen was suddenly at my elbow, guiding me across the vast room. He wore a fine woolen tunic. His face was clean and his hair smoothed. "Are you all right? Ysabella said you were better. We've been very worried."

"A little headache, that is all," I assured him.

"I'm glad. You look . . . well, you look very pretty." His words startled me, but before I could react, he said, "You must meet the abbess." He led me to the far end of the table near the fire, where a woman in nun's garb sat in a large wooden chair. I couldn't see her shape beneath her habit, but it was clear that she was very tall. Under her wimple, her features were sharp, her nose long and aquiline. At first I thought she was young, but when I drew closer, I could see signs of age around her eyes and mouth. As I approached, the abbess put her goblet down. She did not smile.

"Holy Mother," Owen said in French, "may I present Rype?"

Abbess Katharina looked me up and down, pursing her lips. There was a moment of quiet, when the chatter of the others at the table faded away. I could feel my familiar panic begin to rise, and I tried to slow my breath.

"Rype?" she said at last, her French heavily accented. "What sort of name is that?"

I didn't know if I was supposed to speak, but Owen nudged me. "It is … Norwegian, Holy Mother," I said. At least I hoped that's what I had said; my French was very unpracticed.

"Ah," she said, and then, in my language, "And how did you come from Norway to my abbey?" I stared at her. I hadn't heard Norwegian since Owen's father had died.

"You speak my language!" I blurted. Then the abbess did smile.

"Yes, child. I speak eight languages. And Latin, of course."

I bowed to her, full of amazement. A woman who

was more educated than any man I'd ever known—as educated as a king, surely! I began to stammer a reply to the question, but the abbess had lost interest and turned from me to speak to the man sitting on her left.

We made our way to an open place at the table, next to Ysabella and Jacme. I looked around for Raymond and saw him between two lordly looking men, his new embroidered tunic dull beside their gold-threaded robes. He was laughing and talking and eating all at once, clearly at home in this grand company.

The food placed before me was finer than any I had ever tasted. There was meat and fowl, fish and vegetables I could not identify. There were honey cakes and the spring's first strawberries with thick cream. I tasted it all, thinking I would never have another chance to try such wondrous fare. I swallowed blood-red wine, strong and smooth, which went to my head at once. The light-headedness I'd felt from the blow to my head blended with a new dizziness, and the room seemed to sparkle and spin.

"Slowly!" Ysabella cautioned, seeing me wobble on my stool. "You are not used to the wine."

"It tastes of . . . berries," I said, sipping again. "It does not taste like wine at all!" The wine I knew was always sour.

"The abbess has her own vineyards, and her own vintners," Jacme told me, taking a swig from his own gold goblet.

I looked around at the company. There were at least twenty at table, men and women both, all dressed in rich fabrics and unfamiliar styles. Some of the women wore tall headdresses that came to a point, with veils that cascaded down their backs. Some wore dresses cut so low that their bosoms showed, which seemed wrong to me in a religious house. I could not tell if they were truly beautiful, or if it was just the clothes they wore, their elaborate hair and head coverings. But they were a feast for my eyes as the food was for my tongue.

Then the abbess called for music, and Raymond, Ysabella, and Jacme stood and moved to her end of the table. A servant entered, carrying Raymond's lute and Jacme's flute. The gathering kept up their chatter at first, but before long they quieted to hear Ysabella and Raymond sing together, one of their long heroic ballads.

I sat next to a nobleman, with another lord on his far side. Both were middle-aged, obviously wealthy, and not entirely sober. One had a long scar that ran from the top of his cheek to his chin. Whatever battle he'd been in, he had nearly lost his nose. They fixed their eyes on Ysabella and spoke to each other about her in their guttural

German. From the tone of their voices, I was glad not to know what they said. Then one turned to me and said, in French, "She is very beautiful. Is she married to the old man?" He must have meant Raymond.

I shook my head. I did not want to talk to them. I wished Owen would turn and notice, but he was talking to a lady on his other side.

"You are very beautiful as well," the second man said to me. I stared at the table, tracing with my finger the intricate embroidery of the cloth that covered it. The men laughed at my embarrassment.

Raymond and Ysabella sang several songs, and then Ysabella called for me to come and join them. It was only because I wanted to get away from the lords that I jumped from my stool and made my way to the head of the table. I noted Owen's surprised face as I passed, but the wine made me brave.

"Does the wild bird from Norway sing, then?" the abbess asked, in French this time. The lords and ladies laughed. At my blank look, she repeated her question in Norwegian.

"A little, Your Holiness," I murmured.

"Your Holiness! I am not the pope, child," she said, and the others laughed louder.

"If you were the pope, Holy Mother, we would be done with this scourge of Sickness," said a man seated nearby. I hoped I didn't look as shocked as I felt. The idea of a woman as pope, even as a joke—surely the abbess must be appalled!

"Sacrilege, my lord!" the abbess chided him, but she looked pleased at the thought. It was clear that I was completely out of my depth in this company.

Jacme brought me a stool, and I sat beside Ysabella. "Let us sing the one we've been working on," Ysabella said in a low voice. For several nights before we arrived at Essen, around the evening fires, we had been writing a song. In truth, Ysabella had written it, but we had worked out the words and music together. It was short and a little mournful, in a minor key. Raymond played the opening notes, and Ysabella and I began to sing, our voices—Ysabella's high, mine lower—blending just as we'd practiced.

"How long ago I cannot say,
My lover went to war.
I promised him that I would wait—
Alas! I wait no more.

Another came to claim my heart.
I loved the first one best.
But I betrayed my love, alas!
I failed at love's cruel test.

And when my love came home, alas!
With honor to his name,
He'd lost the war that mattered most,
With time—and me—to blame."

I could not have done it if I hadn't had the wine. It was terrifying to sit before that grand, refined audience and sing. I could feel the heat in my face, and at first I had to stare straight at Owen, his encouraging smile giving me courage. But when we were done, the applause of the listeners lifted my heart. I looked around, seeing the faces of the lords and ladies wreathed in smiles. They liked the song—a song I had helped to write!

"Very nice," the abbess said. "Is it a translation of Peirol?"

"No indeed," Raymond said. "It is an original work. Ysabella and Rype wrote it."

The abbess raised one dark eyebrow. "How interesting." She sounded skeptical. "Do they write all your songs?"

Raymond laughed. "No, Holy Mother, I write most of my own songs. But they are troubairitz in their own right."

I was thrilled to be called a troubairitz. I had only written part of one song, and I knew I did not really deserve the name, but still it delighted me.

Another group came up to perform then, and the abbess had Ysabella and me sit beside her, saving the place on her right for Jacme. She did not pay much attention to the new singers but spoke to Jacme in a low voice, smiling in a way that transformed her sharp features nearly to beauty. Ysabella talked with a young, handsome lord next to her, but my French was not good enough for conversation, so mostly I watched. Raymond was quiet too, and I saw him gazing at Jacme and the abbess, his eyes narrowed.

As the excitement of performing wore off, I felt the effects of the wine more strongly, and I began to sway a bit on my stool. I tried to catch Ysabella's eye, to hint to her that it might be time for bed, but Ysabella shook her head and nodded toward her brother. I was confused. It seemed that Ysabella did not want to leave Jacme. Or perhaps we could not leave until the abbess did? The evening wore on and on. My head started to throb again, and I felt quite ill, but still we stayed at table.

At last the performers finished, the carafes of wine were empty, and the abbess stood. When she rose, everyone at the table got to their feet as well.

"Good night, all," the abbess said in French, and she said the same to me in Norwegian. Then she said it again in what must have been German. She kept a hand lightly on Jacme's arm. Ysabella's lips tightened, and Raymond grew pale.

"We shall be more than comfortable in the men's quarters," Raymond said, but his light tone belied the set of his mouth. "Come, Jacme!" But the abbess did not release her hold.

Jacme smiled at Raymond. I could see that his eyes were trying to tell Raymond something, but I could not tell what it was. "I will be along shortly, my friend," he said.

Beside me, Raymond took a deep breath, but before he could speak Ysabella laid a gentle hand on his shoulder. "Do you recall the way to the sleeping quarters?" she asked him. "I am turned around—or perhaps it is the abbess's fine wine that has turned my head!"

The lords and ladies closest, who had been watching the exchange with interest, laughed at this, and bowed to the abbess before they left to retire for the night.

Ysabella and Raymond followed them, and I stumbled behind. Owen came up beside me and steadied me.

"I hope we are only staying one night," he said in a low voice. "We need to get back on the road."

"I'm sorry," I told him. I knew that the delay troubled him greatly. "It's my fault that we had to stay."

"No!" he protested. "You couldn't help it. And besides, Raymond wanted to see the abbess—to make a little money."

In front of us, I could see that Raymond's hands were clenched in fists. We walked in silence past the cloister, through the quiet halls, and then down a new hall into a separate building. There, the men entered one room and the women another. Owen gave a little wave as we separated, but Raymond did not look back.

The ladies' room was long and tiled and lined with beds hung with red velvet drapes and covered with fine blankets. There were at least a dozen beds along the walls. Each had a little table beside it, and a lighted candle stood on each table. Ysabella chose a bed at the end of one wall, giving privacy at least on one side. We took off our kirtles and folded them carefully, then slid into our bed. I blew out the candle, and Ysabella reached out and pulled the drapes closed around us.

"What—?" I began, too curious to hold back.

"Shh!" Ysabella hissed. "Wait until they are asleep."

I was desperately tired, sore and light-headed, but I had to know what had just happened. I kept myself awake by pinching the skin on the inside of my arm until I was sure I was black and blue. Finally the room filled with the soft breathing and light snores of women sleeping, and I poked Ysabella.

"Why did Jacme go with the abbess?" I whispered.

"Why do you think?" Ysabella said. I could not see her face, but even in a whisper her tone was grim.

I knew what I was thinking had to be wrong. "But . . . she is a nun!" I pointed out.

"That means little here," Ysabella replied. "He is a beautiful boy, and she is a very, very powerful woman."

I was silent, pondering this. It was terribly shocking—and yet, having seen the abbess, not entirely unbelievable. "But . . . why was Raymond so upset? Did he and the abbess . . ."

Ysabella snorted. "Oh, my dear," she said. "No. No. It is not like that at all. Raymond is not that way."

I grew more bewildered. "Not what way? What do you mean?"

"Must I explain it to you?"

I was silent.

Ysabella gave a great sigh. "I thought you'd figured it out. Raymond and Jacme—they are together."

"Yes, I know," I said, still not understanding. "We are all together. But why should Raymond mind?"

"*Together,*" Ysabella said again, with emphasis.

I blinked in the darkness. Together? *Together?* I thought of the gentle touches Raymond and Jacme shared. Of the way Raymond called Jacme *mon chéri*. I knew it meant *my dearest.* Or *sweetheart.* "You mean they are . . ."

"Shh," Ysabella cautioned. "Yes. They love each other. And if the abbess knew—if she knew for certain—she would say it is against God's law. She would have them killed."

I drew in a sharp breath. Men who loved other men. I had never known any before. I had heard terrible things about them. But Raymond and Jacme were not like that.

"Go to sleep now," Ysabella said, turning away. "We will leave in the morning—if we can. If the abbess permits."

Father Mathias roars from the pulpit, his pale eyes bulging. "The Sickness is a curse brought down on Skeviga! You have sinned in the eyes of God, and this is your punishment! Leviticus tells us: 'And if you shall despise my statutes, or if your soul abhor my judgments, so that you will not do all my commandments, but that you break my covenant: I also will do this unto you; I will even appoint over you terror, consumption, and the burning ague!'"

Gudrun and I look at each other, wide-eyed. We are petrified. Father Mathias has always been stern, but he is a kind man, a forgiving priest. We have never heard a sermon like this from him before. What loathsome sins had we committed to bring the Sickness down on us?

"'Know you not that the unrighteous shall not inherit the kingdom of God?'" Father Mathias continues, hammering his fist on the pulpit. "'Be not deceived: neither fornicators, nor idolaters, nor adulterers, nor effeminate, nor abusers of themselves with mankind, nor thieves, nor covetous, nor drunkards, nor revilers, nor extortioners, shall inherit the kingdom of God.'"

I don't know what most of those things are. But I know we are not like that. There is no one like that in Skeviga, except for Magnus, who is a drunkard. And he is already dead.

Two days later, Father Mathias dies too.

Chapter Eight

"RYPE!" I HEARD MY NAME WHISPERED, AND I struggled to wake. My head ached, and I was weary through and through.

Someone shook me, and I opened my eyes to see Ysabella. It was still dark in the long room, still silent. "We must go," Ysabella whispered. "The others are outside."

I struggled to rise, and Ysabella helped me dress. We wore the new kirtles; our old ones hadn't been returned to us. The other women in the room slept on, the wine deepening their slumber. We crept out of the room, flinching as the wooden door creaked, and pushed it gently shut behind us. In the dim corridor, I could see the forms of Raymond, Owen, and Jacme. Jacme stood off by himself against the wall, his hood shadowing his face.

"Our horses . . . ?" Ysabella said to Raymond, low.

"In the courtyard," he replied.

Owen took my arm, seeing how shakily I moved, and Ysabella put her arm around Jacme. As quietly as we could, we made our way out of the guesthouse.

"There will be guards," Owen told me. "Follow our lead."

In the courtyard at the front of the abbey, the horses waited quietly at one side. The men took their bridles and moved toward the guardhouse at the entrance. As we approached, Owen and Raymond began to walk unsteadily, acting as if they were drunk. Ysabella did the same. I didn't have to act; my sight was blurred, and I had trouble placing one foot in front of the other.

At the guardhouse, a soldier stood, lance in hand. He looked at us, spat to the side, and laughed. "A long night, eh?" he said.

Raymond pulled his lute off his shoulder, cradling it in his arms. "Ah, my friend, they made us play for hours! And for what reward? A few copper coins, no more."

"Enough to share, I'm sure," the guard said, spitting again.

Raymond shrugged. "If you say so. We can spare a coin."

"Two," the guard said flatly.

Raymond hesitated just long enough, then said, "If you insist." He pulled out two coins from his purse and tossed them, and as the soldier lunged for them we passed through the arch that led to the street outside. We walked more quickly then, not looking behind us, and turned down one street and then another, not stopping until we were sure we were far enough from the abbey to be safe. I leaned on Johann, afraid I might be sick.

"Here, let me help you up," Owen said. He boosted me onto the saddle and swung up behind me. Jacme and Ysabella climbed onto the palfrey, and Raymond mounted Old Man. His shoulders were slumped, as if the scene with the guard had drained him completely.

Wordlessly we wound through the streets of Essen. I had thought it so beautiful when we first came, but now I knew better. The spires of the abbey and the other churches still rose high and white into the lightening sky, but there was a darkness here I couldn't name.

We rode through the city gates, and I was glad to leave. "Lean against me and sleep," Owen said. His arms were strong around me. I leaned back against his chest. It was much nicer than riding with Ysabella.

"Is Jacme all right?" I asked. "And Raymond?"

"They aren't hurt, if that's what you mean," Owen said.

"That is not exactly what I mean."

"So you know . . . ?"

I turned to see his face, wincing as the movement made my head throb. "Now I do. Did you always know?"

He smiled gently at me. "I figured it out. I've been many places, Rype, and seen many things."

"But . . . is it not wrong?"

"The Church says so. I leave that judgment to God."

I thought of what Owen had said to me in the inn a week or more ago. *There are good people and bad, greedy ones and kind ones. Gentle and rough. In every place, there are the same sorts.* If Jacme and Raymond were bad, then what did that make the abbess Katharina? Perhaps what I'd always thought bad and good meant, what I had been taught they meant, wasn't entirely true. But then what *was* true? How could you tell good from bad? My head spun enough without trying to make

sense of that. I decided that I too would leave judgment to God. I leaned against Owen again and closed
my eyes. Johann's gentle *clip-clop* and sway was like a
lullaby, and before long I was asleep.

I woke once when we had to cross a river. There
was a ferry, but it was too small to take the horses.
We rode across. The water was nearly deep enough
to make Old Man swim, and he panicked when he
lost his footing. We all were soaked to the skin in our
efforts to hold him and calm him.

I dried off eventually, but then a gentle, misting
rain began. We pulled up our hoods and went on. The
rain kept up for days, the sky dour and gray. It was too
damp to kindle a fire. The weather seemed to match
everyone's mood. Nobody smiled; we only spoke when
we had to. There was no music of an evening, even
when we found shelter. Jacme's eyes were shadowed.
Ysabella stayed close to him, but Raymond ignored
him completely.

"Why is Raymond being so unkind?" I asked Owen
one afternoon when we had fallen behind the others
far enough not to be overheard.

"He is hurt, can't you see that?" Owen said.

"Of course I can. But it isn't fair, is it? What would
have happened if Jacme had not gone with the abbess?"

"I don't know. I don't think we'd have fared well."

"Then he did what he had to, didn't he? He may even have saved us."

"Reason can't reason with love," Owen said. "Have you never been in love?"

I blushed. It was the same question Ysabella had asked me. "Never," I answered, low.

Owen smiled. "There will be plenty of time for that," he said. "You will fall in love with an English boy from Gravesend, and I will make sure that he is good enough for you." He pulled my braid gently, and I smiled back.

I distracted myself from my headache by thinking of what Owen had said about his home, his family. Of living in a town, in a house with no fields or animals to tend. Of having a new mother, a new sister. Even of falling in love with an English boy. It was all hard to imagine. I didn't know what they ate in Gravesend or what kind of clothes they wore. Surely they had different feast days and different traditions than we'd had in Skeviga. It would be hard to learn a whole life anew—but Owen would be with me. If we could get there. If his mother and little Alice were still alive.

The rain finally let up, though the sun was veiled.

The road from Essen was wide, and as we drew closer to the city of Liège, we began to see peasants toiling in the fields, and traders and merchants heading toward the city. Most of the travelers moved along the road a little faster than we did, held back as we were by Old Man's advanced age. We had to scramble off the road for one group that came up behind us in a great hurry, two well-dressed mounted men flanking a cart drawn by two trotting horses. They shouted to Raymond to get out of the way, and I saw, as they sped by, the scar that slashed across the face of one. It was the same man who had sat beside me at dinner in Essen. For a moment I was frightened, and I could see the same fear in Jacme's and Ysabella's faces.

"Those men were in Essen," I said to Ysabella.

"Yes, I remember them," she replied. "I was afraid—"

"It is good the abbess doesn't search for us," Raymond interrupted, coming up beside us. He dismounted from Old Man. "I think we should give this ancient fellow a rest and walk for a time. I need to stretch my legs." He extended a hand to Jacme, who gave him a searching look, then took his hand and slid down from the palfrey. They walked on, leading Old Man. Ysabella, Owen, and I got off as well and walked behind. I could see Jacme's dark head bent to Raymond's lighter one as we moved along. I was so glad they were speaking again—their unhappiness had bled into everything.

We reached a village before night, and some of the villagers invited us to stay. The family seemed healthy, and they spoke French, so we accepted the invitation. A barn was provided for the horses with a loft for us, and we joined a group of village families at their evening meal. It was simple food, pottage and ale, but it was good and flavored with a bit of meat and new greens. We ate our fill, and then we played and sang for the whole village. I sang my song with Ysabella again, this time with more confidence and less wine in me. Having people's eyes on me did not bother me as much now when I performed. When I stopped, and they clapped or cheered, I could feel my cheeks heat and I wanted to disappear. But the singing . . . I was growing to enjoy that.

The weather warmed and warmed. The trees were in full leaf now. The world, it seemed, had come back to life. People tilled the fields. The familiar signs of death and ruin that had been all around diminished as we came closer to the city.

I hadn't realized that we'd been climbing as we followed the road through the woods, past farms and fields. But we came out suddenly on a wide plateau, high above what Raymond told us was the River Meuse. The sky overhead was a golden gray, with scudding clouds that opened for a moment to let the sun's rays flood the valley below before they closed again, shutting out the light as if God had blown out a candle. On one side rose the city walls, which descended the steep hill all the way to the river, enclosing the city within. Below, the river snaked along, its waters dividing to surround an island in its center and then meeting again. The island too was walled.

"The city is very well defended," Owen said, impressed.

"Their ruler is a prince and a bishop, both," Raymond told him. "But the real power in the city is the guilds. It is not like most other places. The merchants run Liège, and they like a nice thick wall, the fat fools. It makes them feel safe."

"Do you look down on the merchants, then?" Ysabella teased him. "But you come from merchant stock yourself."

Raymond smiled, a little sourly. "My fortunes are linked with the nobles, my friend, as are yours. No flabby mason or soot-smeared blacksmith or rank fishmonger would hire a troubadour. They are men who think of only two things: their money and their meals.

Music means little to them. But the prince-bishop still holds sway here, and he is my patron's good friend."

"Your patron knows everyone, it seems," I said, thinking of the abbess.

"He is a very powerful man, the Duke of Burgundy," Raymond replied.

"Well," said Owen, "I hope the prince-bishop is less ... difficult than the abbess." Raymond looked sharply at him, but then he chuckled.

"Let us hope he likes us a little less," he agreed. I did not dare look at Jacme.

"Raymond . . . ," Owen said, his voice hesitant. "I've been thinking that maybe Rype and I should continue on and not stop here in Liège. The journey is so long, and I fear for my family, alone at home." He turned to me. "If you agree."

I nodded, and Raymond pursed his lips. "I understand, my friend," he said. "Truly I do. And of course, you are free to go on alone if you wish. But I am hoping for an escort, or a guarantee of safe passage, from the prince-bishop. It is possible that we will move more swiftly if that happens."

I looked at Owen. His face was so open; I could see the feelings move across it like wind on water. Worry, hope, fear—how could he make such a decision?

"We have to sleep somewhere," Owen said at last. "And if you think there is a chance of more safety and a faster passage from Liège, I must take it." He sighed, and we started our descent to the city.

The light faded as we approached the walls, but we reached the gate before nightfall. The guards stopped us, laughing at the instruments we carried.

"The prince-bishop is far too holy for your music, Troubadour!" one of them said to Raymond. He spoke in French. I was able to understand most of what he said now.

"We can be as holy as he requires," Raymond replied.

"I doubt that," the guard said. "We are required by law to ask: Have you any signs of the Sickness? Any swellings, fever, shortness of breath?"

"We are in good health," Raymond assured him, and though the guard looked us over suspiciously, he finally waved us through.

The streets were a maze. Once we were inside the wall, it was impossible to see the spires of the prince-bishop's palace or the cathedral, so we walked aimlessly, stopping now and then to ask directions. At last the warren of streets opened onto an enormous square, empty but for a few monks scurrying across, their dark robes brushing the cobblestones. At the far end of the square was the palace. Next to it a towering cathedral stood, one stone spire rising high. The other was under construction; it rose only half as tall as the finished one, and scaffolding covered it. Two sides of the square held buildings at right angles, and it was to the closer of those structures that Raymond headed.

"I had a friend at the abbey here once," Raymond said. "Brother Bernard. I haven't seen him in—oh, decades. But if he still lives, he'll welcome us, I'm sure."

Jacme dismounted and rang the bell at the monastery door. It was only a moment before the door creaked open, and a red-haired, tonsured monk peered out.

"Is there a Brother Bernard here?" Raymond asked.

The monk pursed his lips. "There are three Brothers Bernard. And our abbot's name is Bernard."

Raymond snorted. "Don't you have any other names here in Liège? I don't know which one he would be. He was born in Dijon."

The monk nodded. "That would be Abbot Bernard, then."

Raymond raised an eyebrow. "*Mon Dieu!* I would not have guessed he'd rise so high!"

"He is a very holy and righteous man," the monk said, and Raymond bit his lip.

"May we have an audience, then? I am his old friend Raymond of Dijon, you can tell him. I think he will remember me."

The monk hesitated, then opened the door wider. "Tie your horses, and then sit inside," he said, motioning to a bench in the long stone hallway. "I'll be back shortly."

Jacme tied up the horses, and we sat on the wooden bench, grateful for a seat that didn't sway and bounce under us. The hall was silent. Even the occasional passing monks seemed to move soundlessly, a sidelong glance in our direction the only acknowledgment they gave. It was far different from Abbess Katharina's bustling convent.

At last the red-haired monk reappeared, walking swiftly. "The abbot will see you in his chambers," he said to Raymond. He seemed surprised, and more than a little displeased.

We followed the monk through the halls and up a flight of stone stairs to a thick wooden door. A quick rap was followed by the command "Enter!" The monk held the door open, then stood aside as we passed through.

I looked around with curiosity. The room was large and very plain. Its floor was stone; its furnishings were a table and a high-backed chair. An enormous silver cross holding a carved silver Jesus hung above the fireplace—the room's only decoration. Candles flickered in a half-dozen silver candle holders; night had fallen outside.

The man seated behind the table wore a tall, ornate hat of dark-green velvet and a patterned red robe. His face was round and plump and unwrinkled. One of his hands, clasped on the table, sported a ring with a huge red stone.

Raymond bowed, and quickly the rest of us followed suit. "Father Abbot," Raymond said. "We are your most humble servants."

The abbot looked at us without speaking, and the silence stretched until I began to feel very uncomfortable.

We all jumped when the abbot burst into laughter. He slapped his hand onto the tabletop and cried out, "Raymond, you rogue, you never sent a letter, after all your promises! I thought you were long dead. How grand to see you in the flesh!"

"Not dead yet," Raymond said, grinning. "And my flesh doesn't begin to compete with yours. I take it that the meals here at Saint-Laurent are hearty!"

The abbot laughed and patted his stomach. "Indeed

they are, my friend. Would you expect otherwise, with me in charge?"

"And would you, in the way of Saint Benedict, share your bounty with pilgrims?"

"Are you a pilgrim, then, Raymond? I must hear about this. I'll call for a meal, and you can take it here with me, you and your friends." His gaze moved over us, and Raymond introduced us. I had never been in the presence of such an exalted cleric before. This abbot looked as I imagined the pope might look, with his elegant robes and clean, smooth skin.

The abbot called for food, and it wasn't long before the same monk brought in a platter piled high with meat and bread and a jug of wine. Behind him followed three younger monks, one carrying earthenware plates and mugs, the other two struggling with a wooden bench. Silently the monks placed food on the plates and poured out wine, and the abbot indicated we should sit on the bench.

When the monks had closed the door behind them, Abbot Bernard took up a chop and gnawed on it. We followed suit. The meat was delicious, thickly cut and juicy. It was a rare treat for us.

"I see you flaunt the Rule forbidding meat," Raymond observed between bites. "And lamb, no less!"

"The Rule forbids meat in the refectory, not in the abbot's chambers," the abbot protested. "I am a good Benedictine. Better than you ever were, that is certain."

My eyes widened. Raymond had been a monk? I caught Owen's eye; he looked as startled as I felt. I hadn't known a man could be a monk and then stop being one. I'd thought those vows were for life. But Raymond rarely did what other people did.

Raymond noticed the look on my face, and he smiled. "Yes, I once thought to become a monk, Little Bird," he said. "But it was the music I loved, not the life there. I could not give my heart to God in the way a monk must. So I left the abbey and went to court, and I became a musician."

"Best for the abbey, if not for your soul," the abbot said, chuckling. "Ah, Raymond, my friend, do you remember when you put the beetle in the hollowed-out apple at supper in the refectory?"

Raymond spat out a mouthful of food with his hoot of laughter. "Indeed I do! Imagine this, you three—there the apple, sitting like an ordinary piece of fruit on a table, and suddenly the beetle inside begins to wander about, and makes the apple roll from side to side as if it had a mind of its own. I well recall Abbot

Pierre's terrified prayers when he thought it was possessed by the devil!"

We listened enthralled as the two men told stories about their time together in an abbey in the east of France, where they had grown up and taken holy vows together. Raymond had been a troublemaker even then; another tale had him hiding a dead mouse in the abbot's bed, and in still another, he set a pot full of urine to cook in the fireplace, and when the smell emptied out the kitchen, he stole the pear tart the cellarer had made. As the wine in the abbot's jug grew lower, the stories grew louder and more raucous. I could hardly believe an abbot would talk about such things, but by the time they ran out of tales, I was giggling with the others.

"Has the Sickness been hard on Liège?" Raymond asked when the lamb had been reduced to a pile of bones. The lightheartedness faded from the abbot's face.

"We've had none in the abbey, thanks be to God, but the town . . . ah, it was terrible last summer. Not much during the winter, but I've heard reports of it returning. I think perhaps the heat of the summer makes it worse."

"I've thought as much myself," Raymond said.

"And you are going south?" Abbot Bernard asked. "Into the heat?"

Raymond shrugged. "We are going south, and we must get this lad to Marseille," he said, motioning to Owen. "He needs a ship to England."

"England!" the abbot exclaimed. "Why do you go so far?"

Raymond nodded at Owen, and he explained his situation to the abbot.

"And the others?" Abbot Bernard asked when he finished.

"Ysabella and Jacme are my companions," Raymond said. "And Rype—well, Rype is from the North, beyond the sea. Her people all died of the Sickness."

The abbot met my eyes, and the sorrow in his surprised me nearly as much as his stories had.

"I am sorry," he said. "For both of you. It is hard, to be left without parents at such a tender age. I have seen it happen too many times, these two years past. We will do what we can to help you on your way."

"Thank you, Father Abbot," Owen said, and I echoed him with a whispered "Thank you."

"Brother Marco!" the abbot called, and immediately the door opened and the red-headed monk entered.

"Our guests are full and sleepy. Take them to their rooms."

"Yes, Father Abbot," Brother Marco said, bowing. He didn't seem pleased at the order, any more than he had been at allowing us inside or feeding us.

"Brother Raymond," the abbot said, "I take it you want to see our prince?"

"That was my intention," Raymond said, standing and stretching. "I hope that he will . . . endow us a bit, for our journey. Or even provide an escort."

"And you didn't ask me for help first?" Abbot Bernard said. He frowned, but his eyes were twinkling.

"I know you too well," Raymond said. "You've taken a vow of poverty—I'm sure that while you have plenty to eat, you have no money to spare. Though I believe one of those candlesticks could pay our entire way to the coast."

Brother Marco drew in a sharp breath at Raymond's disrespectful tone, but the abbot gave his great laugh and slapped his hand on the table again.

"You *bricon*, you do know me!" he boomed. "But the candlesticks—and the cross—were an offering from our wealthiest patron. He is a wool trader—thus our supper lamb, for it is lambing season, and he is a charitable man. But if he were to visit and find his gifts missing . . . well, I wouldn't want to risk his displeasure. It's due to his great generosity that we have enough mutton and lamb to feed our visitors."

"Then we shall leave his candlesticks, and may they help to light your way to Heaven," Raymond said. "For surely you will need all the light you can get!" Again the monk gasped with outrage, and his stride as he led us out of the abbot's office and down the hallway was so fast that I had to jog to keep up.

We passed the night in empty monks' cells. The cots were narrow, but the blankets were soft and warm and there were straw-stuffed pillows. I had never seen a pillow before. When Ysabella explained its use, I was amazed.

"It's just for your head?" I said, stretching out on the cot with my head on the pillow. "Oh, it does feel nice!"

"Sometimes they stink, but these are nice and fresh," Ysabella said from her cot. "I always sleep better with a pillow. But who can afford them?"

"Someone with a wealthy patron in the wool business," I said, and Ysabella snorted.

"What a constant surprise our Raymond is!" she noted. "I thought I knew everything about him, but I certainly didn't know he was once a monk."

"Is there anything he has not done?" I asked.

"Let me think . . . I don't believe he's ever fought in a battle. And I know for a fact that he can't swim."

"Even I can swim," I said, surprised.

"You are from a fishing village. He is from an inland town. I had to rescue him once when our boat foundered on the Thames, in England. He almost pulled me under. He was deathly afraid."

I found it hard to imagine Raymond being afraid. But the talk had reminded me of the sights and smells of my own village, and I lay long awake, with the scents of salt and sand and fish in my nose and images of sunlight dancing on shushing waves behind my closed eyelids.

I wake alone. I have been alone for a long time. I am so cold. The fire is dead. Everyone, everything, is dead. When I push the door open against the snow that has fallen, the village is silent. Even the birds do not sing. The only footprints in the snow are mine. I have been to all the cottages, taken all the food I can find. There is nothing left. I find myself talking to Gudrun, to Sigrid. To Mama, to Per. Nobody answers, of course. I am the only person left in the world.

Chapter Nine

"WHAT DO WE CALL THE PRINCE-BISHOP?"
I asked as Ysabella pulled a comb through my knotted
hair.

Ysabella paused. "That's a good question. Is he Your
Highness, as a prince would be? Or Your Excellency,
as a bishop would be?"

"Your Excellent Highness," I suggested. "Your
High Excellency?"

Ysabella laughed. "I think we'll just let Raymond
do the talking, as usual." Expertly she wove my hair
into a braid and tied the end with a piece of ribbon
that she pulled from her bodice. "There. You look
quite presentable."

"So do you," I said. Of course, Ysabella always looked beautiful, but she had done a little extra primping. She wore the kirtle she'd been given in Essen, which left her delicate shoulder blades uncovered, and her dark curls were crowned with a velvet band embroidered with vivid flowers.

Ysabella curtsied. "Thank you, milady," she said, and I giggled at the address.

We ventured out into the hall and met Owen, Jacme, and Raymond. Raymond and Owen looked rested, but Jacme's eyes were still shadowed and he had a scowl on his handsome face. Ysabella put an arm around him.

"What ails you, brother?" she asked. "Was the pillow too soft for you? The bedclothes too warm?"

"The fleas were too hungry," Jacme said. "I itch from neck to knees. And the place looks so clean!"

"It only takes one flea to make a night miserable," Ysabella said. "Poor boy! Perhaps Abbot Bernard's infirmarian will have something to soothe you."

"Don't mention it to the abbot," Jacme said. "He would be embarrassed. He was a good host."

Raymond laughed. "Oh, I would love to embarrass him!" But Jacme shook his head stubbornly.

We went to morning mass with the monks. Brother

Marco, as unfriendly as the day before, motioned to us afterward, and we followed him to the abbot's office.

"I hope you slept well, my friends," Abbot Bernard said. I saw Ysabella smother a grin and pinch Jacme, but he ignored her.

"Very well indeed, Father Abbot!" Raymond said. "We thank you for your hospitality. Your monks have been very kind—though that one is a bit gloomy." He motioned to the door, behind which, I was sure, Brother Marco lurked.

Abbot Bernard shook his head. "Brother Marco is a woeful case. He was brought to us ill and suffering last year. Not the Sickness, but a terrible fever. He'd lost everyone—much like you, Rype. But unlike you, though he survived, he has turned inward and allowed his loss to sour him and make him fearful. Every night he screams with nightmares. And he especially fears strangers, whom he feels might bring the Sickness into Saint-Laurent. I am hopeful that days spent here, with the care of his fellow monks and the love of God, will ease his terrors over time."

The abbot's eyes were sad, and my own eyes stung at his kindness. What a contradiction he was! Godly, yet profane in his stories; rough and rude with his old friend, yet as gentle as a doe with his monks. I was beginning to believe that people were often not just good or bad. Many of them seemed to be a mix, good and bad stirred together in a sort of human pottage.

"I think Brother Marco will get better here," I said in my halting French. The abbot smiled at me, then rubbed his hands together.

"So! I have sent word to our prince-bishop that you would like to meet with him, and he has sent a message back. He will see you after dinner and before prayers at None. And he would like you to perform for him."

Raymond's eyebrows went up. "Indeed! And what do you think we should perform, Father Abbot?"

"Let me see . . . 'Confession of Golias,' perhaps?"

Jacme snorted, and Raymond laughed. "Or 'Welcome, Bacchus,' if we're going in that direction?"

I didn't know the words to "Confession of Golias," but I knew "Welcome, Bacchus," a song so bawdy that we only played it in taverns after any women and children had gone to bed. But the abbot laughed his great laugh and said, "I believe that '*Alma Redemptoris Mater*' would be more to His Excellency's taste."

Raymond smiled. "That tells me all I need to know."

"He does love music, Prince-Bishop Englebert, as long as it has a religious theme. And he is a great bene-factor of our local musicians," Abbot Bernard said. "If

you don't slip up and sing 'If a boy with a girl / tarries
in a little room, / happy is their coupling' by accident,
you may do very well with him." Raymond hooted,
and I felt my cheeks redden as I held back a laugh.

"Brother Marco will show you where to go. Good
luck to you, my friends! Raymond, I do beg you to
send word sometime, though I think you will not."

"Probably not," Raymond admitted. "My fingers
want to write only music. But you never know."

"God be with you, all!"

"And with you," we responded. Brother Marco,
obviously listening at the door, opened it wide, and
we filed out.

Wordlessly, Brother Marco led us to the refectory,
where we took a large but silent meal with the other
brothers. Then we gathered up our belongings and
followed the sullen monk out the great door of the
monastery. He pointed across the square to the prince-
bishop's palace.

"Our horses," Raymond said. "Are they stabled?"

Brother Marco nodded.

"We will get them after we have seen His Excellency, then. Thank you for your . . . hospitality."

Again the monk nodded, ignoring Raymond's ironic
tone. I remembered what the abbot had told us about

Brother Marco's family and looked at him with sympathy, but he scowled at me. I turned away. It was hard to feel sorry for someone so closed off. I knew what he suffered in his heart, but I was glad my own losses hadn't made me that bitter.

We walked across the square, crowded now with people on their way to or from market or the shops in the alleys that branched from the central plaza. There were monks everywhere, it seemed, and nuns too, going in and out of the cathedral. Men and women in fine robes and kirtles walked across the cobblestones with purpose. It was a very grand square. But I noticed a cluster of people in rougher clothes sitting against the wall of the cathedral across from the palace. I could see how those passing the group gave them a wide berth, and even from a distance I made out the telltale pallor of their faces. They were ill.

The abbot was wrong: The Sickness sat just outside his doors.

I hurried after the others as they walked up the wide stone steps to the palace entrance. A series of columns ran the length of the enormous building, and two guards stood at attention between the center columns, their armor glinting in the sun, their lances crossed.

"Who wishes to enter?" one of them demanded.

"Raymond the troubadour and his people," Raymond said. "We have an appointment with His Excellency."

The guard motioned to a boy standing just inside the entrance, and the boy ran into the building to announce our arrival.

"Show your necks," the guard instructed us.

It took me a moment to understand that he wanted to make sure we didn't have an early sign of the Sickness—the swelling of the neck. Ysabella and I loosened the tops of our cloaks and exposed our necks, and Raymond and Jacme removed their hoods. The guard looked at us closely, then grunted his approval.

The boy came running back, and the guard motioned to us to follow him. We passed under the crossed lances and into the palace.

"Leave your bags," the boy instructed us. Quickly we piled our bags in a small room just off the entrance. Raymond put down his lute, but the boy said, "Bring your instruments!"

I could hardly take in all I saw as we hurried down the hallway and up a short flight of stairs. The floors were smooth stone, the windows tall and pointed. The walls were hung with bright tapestries, even more elaborate than the ones at the convent in Essen. They showed all manner of scenes: saints in churches and soldiers in battle, and one, I was sure as we trotted past, was of Noah and his animals in the great ark. I wanted to stop at each, to marvel at the intricately woven figures, the plants and beasts crowded into each scene. Even the ceilings were glorious, painted with stars and flowers and cherubs.

"You'll swallow a fly!" Ysabella whispered to me, and I realized my mouth was open with wonder. Owen, too, was staring. The others, no doubt, had seen such marvels before, but I could hardly believe that the same kind of weaving I'd once done at home, on the little loom beside the smoking fireplace of my family's cottage, could produce something as magnificent as those tapestries.

We entered the Great Hall then, and it was even more overwhelming. Guards stood at attention along each of the walls, which were hung with still more tapestries. At the far end, a fire blazed in an enormous fireplace. The hearth was topped with an elaborate chimneypiece depicting carved stone deer meeting in combat, their antlers intertwined. High windows inlaid with stained glass left squares of color on the floor where the sun shone through. I breathed in the scent of incense, remembering to keep my mouth closed despite my awe.

"He has the wealth of both a prince and a bishop," Raymond whispered. "Twice as much of everything."

Before the grand fireplace, a man sat in an oversize upholstered wooden chair. He wore a bishop's miter, rising high above his brow, and a bishop's robes of dark red, with a white cross embroidered down the center. Unlike Abbot Bernard, he was thin beneath his robes, his face drawn downward in a frown.

We walked to within a few yards of the chair and sank into deep bows. When we rose, the prince-bishop's expression had not changed.

"Your Excellency, I bring you greetings from Odo, Duke of Burgundy," Raymond said.

The prince-bishop nodded. "Ah," he said. "And how does your lord Odo?"

"I have not seen him these many months, but I hope he fares well."

"There has been little news out of Dijon," the prince-bishop said. "I know the Sickness was strong there in the autumn. But I am sure I would have heard if he had died." He made the sign of the cross, and Raymond did the same.

"You are a bit earlier than I had hoped," the prince-bishop went on. "But I thought rather than keep you waiting, I would listen a bit to your music before you perform for my guests."

Raymond blinked, surprised. "Are we performing for guests, Your Excellency?" he asked. "We would be honored, of course—but who is our audience?"

Prince-Bishop Englebert's frown deepened. "I assumed that Abbot Bernard would have told you. The pope's own envoy, Bishop Denis, comes to us today. He is fond of music, as our Holy Father Pope Clement is, so at Abbot Bernard's urging, we have invited you to play for him."

"That gouty knave Bernard!" Raymond muttered. "He never said a word to me about this!"

"Pardon?" the prince-bishop said.

Raymond cleared his throat. "We are honored. It is a privilege, to be sure."

There was a little grouping of benches to the prince-bishop's left, and we arranged ourselves there. Raymond sat with his lute, Jacme with his flute, and Owen with the tabor. Ysabella and I stood in front of them. When the prince-bishop nodded, Raymond struck a chord, and we sang, doing our best to look devout.

"Creator-spirit, all-Divine,
Come, visit every soul of thine,
And fill with thy celestial flame
The hearts which thou thyself didst frame."

I was glad Ysabella had chosen to keep her cloak on; the tight kirtle would not have pleased the prince-bishop, I was sure. And a papal envoy would likely be even stricter about what was proper. When we had finished all the verses, the prince-bishop clasped his hands together, and his mouth pulled itself up into a smile.

"I have only heard monks chant '*Veni Creator Spiritus*,'" he said. "It was beautiful even then, but your voices and instruments make it truly sublime."

"We are glad it pleases Your Excellency," Raymond said, and we bowed our heads.

There was a knock at the door, and a guard opened it. The boy who had brought us into the palace entered and bowed before the prince-bishop.

"Your Excellency," he said, "the papal envoy is approaching the city gates."

The prince-bishop sighed deeply. I wondered, from that sigh, if he was unhappy about having to host the pope's envoy. He rose and clapped his hands, and the guards who stood along the walls arranged themselves in two lines. The prince-bishop walked between the two rows, beckoning to us to follow him. Outside the room, the hallway was crowded with monks and prelates who lined up behind the prince-bishop as he walked toward the entrance. In the throng I saw Abbot Bernard, closely flanked by Brother Marco. Raymond saw him too, and shook his fist in the abbot's direction, and the abbot laughed.

Just at the palace door, a priest stopped the prince-bishop. With a few muttered words in Latin, the priest draped an extravagant robe of ermine-trimmed cloth of gold around the prince-bishop's shoulders and then stood aside so he could pass.

"What is happening?" I whispered to Raymond.

"The papal envoy will be greeted at the city gates," Raymond told me. "He is the pope's own representative and must be treated as if he were the pope himself. It is a very formal occasion."

We marched through the streets of Liège as onlookers stared, until we reached the main gates. In the distance, I could see a similarly long line of people making their way down the road toward the city, some on horseback, some on foot. As they came closer,

I noticed that the first man in the line was a priest carrying a white cross almost as tall as he was. Behind him rode a short, very round man wearing a scarlet robe trimmed with ermine and a matching broad-brimmed hat.

"The one in the hat is the envoy," Raymond said, low.

The envoy dismounted, and Prince-Bishop Engle-bert walked up to him and knelt. The envoy held out his hand, and the prince-bishop kissed his ring as a group of monks began to sing.

Raymond winced. "That baritone is out of tune," he murmured.

"Hush!" Jacme warned, jabbing him with an elbow.

When the monks had finished, the prince-bishop spoke. "Your Excellency," he said, "we welcome you to Liège and hope your stay here is everything you could wish."

"I, Bishop Denis of Avignon, bring you greetings from His Holiness Pope Clement," the envoy replied. His voice was so unexpectedly high and squeaky that I had the urge to laugh. I heard Raymond snort. The envoy handed a scroll to the prince-bishop, who unrolled it, scanned it briefly, and handed it to one of his servants.

"Please enter our city," the prince-bishop said. "We are honored to have the ambassador of His Holiness the Pope with us. We offer you our hospitality and our devotion."

The envoy walked forward, and we stood aside as he and his entourage paraded through the gates. A group of priests followed him, and behind them came monks, and then soldiers, ten in all. At the end of the group came servants, all male, and mules carrying supplies.

We fell in line with the prince-bishop's people behind the envoy's, and we all trooped back through the town to the palace. Many of the townspeople bowed low as we passed, but some of them were chatting together, and children played in the alleys. I realized that the people of Liège must be used to such ceremonial events.

At the palace, most of the envoy's people went off to the stables or their rooms. The envoy walked with Prince-Bishop Englebert to the Great Hall, and the prince-bishop motioned to us to follow him. In the Hall, the prince-bishop bowed again to Bishop Denis and said, "We offer you wine, and a musical interlude as you rest from your journey." He motioned, and a servant came forward with a goblet that the prince-bishop took from his hand and gave to the envoy.

A second, slightly smaller chair had been brought in, but Bishop Denis walked forward without hesitating and sat in the prince-bishop's grand chair. For a moment the prince-bishop stood still, his eyebrows raised. Again I wanted to laugh. I imagined these two eminent men coming to blows over who got to sit in the chair, who was more important—hats flying off, rolling on the floor in their elegant robes. I had to bite my lip hard to keep the giggles in. Next to me, I could feel Raymond quivering, and I moved away from him so he wouldn't set me off. The room was very, very quiet.

After an awkward pause, the prince-bishop graciously allowed the envoy to remain seated. When he turned to us, though, his lips were pressed together tightly.

"What would you play for our esteemed guest?" he asked.

"'*Ave Domina*,' may it please Your Excellencies," Raymond replied. The prince-bishop nodded and sat in the smaller chair, and Raymond played a series of chords. I gasped; it was the beginning of "Welcome,

Bacchus," the bawdy tavern song. I closed my eyes, waiting for him to start singing, for the offended shouts to rise up, for us to be thrown out of the palace or imprisoned for impiety. But Raymond kept playing, shifting into the tune of "*Ave Domina*," his face solemn. I was so startled that I missed my opening, but Raymond had obviously expected this reaction to his joke, so he played the introduction again. This time I was prepared.

"Worshipped be the birth of thee;
Quem portasti Maria.
Both in village and in city.
Ave Domina.
For through our sins we were forlorn
Infernali pena
He shall us save whom thou hast borne,
Ave Domina!"

Ysabella and I traded off each second line, with Raymond and Jacme coming in on the Latin phrases and Owen's tabor sounding a steady beat. Our voices blended together and rose in the great room. I stole a glance at the envoy. His eyes were closed, and a small smile played on his lips.

When we were finished, there was a moment of silence. Then the envoy opened his eyes and took a sip of his wine. "Lovely," he murmured. "'*Ave Domina.*' May we hear more?"

"They will perform this evening, when we have concluded our business," Prince-Bishop Englebert said. "If that is to Your Excellency's liking?"

"Very much so," the envoy replied. He rose, and a servant rushed forward to take him to his room.

The prince-bishop turned to us. "You will stay," he said. It was not a question. "We will provide room and food for you, and tonight you will play again. I assume you have a repertoire of holy songs?"

"Of course," Raymond said smoothly. I knew this wasn't really true; the two we had performed were the only ones we had practiced. Still, Raymond didn't seem worried; we had a few hours to work.

Our rooms were in the servants' wing of the palace, but they were still far more luxurious than anything I had ever experienced. The beds had pillows stuffed with feathers, not straw, and the mattresses too were feather. Ysabella and I lay back on the bed, groaning with delight.

"It's like lying on a cloud!" Ysabella cried. "Oh, we shall sleep tonight!"

The room itself was nearly as large as my whole cottage in Skeviga had been. There were half a dozen candles in silver holders, and an enormous wooden cupboard to store our belongings. A window looked out on the palace's central courtyard. I got up from the bed and stood staring down at the comings and goings below; it was nearly as busy as the square in front of the cathedral had been. What did all those people do? I wondered. Where were they from, where were they going?

Ysabella interrupted my reverie. "We must practice," she said, taking my arm. "We haven't very long to learn a lot of new songs!"

Raymond, Jacme, and Owen were in the next room; we could hear the sound of the lute through the thick wooden door. We hurried next door and perched on the soft bed.

"Raymond, I thought I would fall over when you started playing 'Welcome, Bacchus,'" Ysabella said, and Raymond let loose with his bellowing laugh.

"It was a little joke, just for us," he said. "It nearly undid Rype, did it not?" I flushed, embarrassed, but

Raymond clapped me on the shoulder, and I had to laugh too.

"Now, we must put religious lyrics to the tunes we know already," Raymond said. "Here, I've written out the words for you." He gave me a sheet of parchment.

"I can't read that!" I said, panicked.

"Just follow me," Ysabella told me. "Your memory is good. You'll remember the words when we say them."

We practiced for hours. Every now and then a servant would poke his nose into the room, drawn by the sound. By the time we felt ready, we had an audience of a dozen, including five soldiers. Our last song, a lyric about the Crucifixion set to the melancholy tune of "Bird on a Briar," left tears in the eyes of even the armed men.

The prince-bishop sent a meal in to us, fine meats and wine. Only Raymond was able to eat. I was so tense that Ysabella had to keep reminding me to breathe. By the time we were called down to the Great Hall, my nerves were thrumming like the lute. Darkness had fallen, and the Hall was lighted with torches and candelabra, the glimmering light reflected in the colored panes of window glass. It was not as beautiful a room as the Hall in the abbey at Essen—it was plainer, less elegant. But still, it was a breathtaking sight. The figures in the tapestries on the walls seemed to move in the flickering glow of the candles. A long table, scattered with the remains of a hearty feast, had been laid in the center of the room. The envoy sat at one end and the prince-bishop at his right. Servants poured more wine as Raymond and Owen took their seats and the rest of us arranged ourselves to the side, so the listeners could see everyone. Raymond struck a chord, and we began.

There was no chatter here, as there had been at the convent in Essen. The entire company was silent as we sang, of the Virgin Mary and her vision of the angel Gabriel, of the birth of Jesus and his death and resurrection. I lost myself in the sacred music. For the first time performing, I wasn't aware of the audience; I felt no shyness or hesitation. My voice rang out strong and true, blending with Ysabella's high tones and Raymond's low ones. And when we finished, the envoy stood and bowed to us, startling the prince-bishop almost as much as it startled us. Quickly Prince-Bishop Englebert stood too.

"Your music has the touch of the divine in it, truly," Bishop Denis said in his funny, high-pitched voice. "I am no admirer of vulgar troubadour tunes, but your songs are both melodious and godly. I am quite amazed."

For once, Raymond was speechless.

"Troubadours, I would ask that my lord, His Holiness the Pope, hear you play. Will you accompany me back to Avignon?"

Raymond looked at Prince-Bishop Englebert, who nodded his head very slightly.

"We would be honored, Your Excellency," Raymond said. "It would be a privilege to play for His Holiness."

Dawn light was coming through the windows of our room by the time Ysabella and I collapsed in exhaustion on our feather bed. "We are going to Avignon!" Ysabella said. "It is near to Le Puy, and we will have a papal envoy and his guards to take us!"

"So . . . that is good news?" I asked doubtfully. "Are we to become servants to the pope?"

"Oh, I don't think so," Ysabella replied. "Raymond is already servant to the Duke of Burgundy. He couldn't serve the pope as well."

"But . . . the pope is a higher lord, isn't he? If he wanted us to work for him, could we say no?"

"Raymond could." Ysabella sounded very certain, but I was not so sure. I had never been anyone's servant, and I did not want to be.

"What of Owen?" I asked. "He will not want to be delayed."

"I don't think it will delay us, to travel with the envoy. They should move quickly, if they have no other stops to make."

"Even with so many people?" I was unconvinced.

Ysabella raised herself on an elbow. "You are very concerned about Owen," she noted.

"He is my friend."

"But . . . more than that?" Ysabella pressed.

I bit my lip. "Are you asking about love again? I don't know. How do you know if you love someone?"

Ysabella lay back again. "Well, I can tell you how *I* know. When I'm in love, my heart thrums like a lute to see him." Her voice grew dreamy. "I want to be with him all the time. Everything is *more*—my happiness is happier, and my sadness is sadder. And of course, my jealousy is very jealous indeed." She laughed. "Is that what you feel?"

"No," I said. "Some of it, perhaps. I want to be with Owen. I like to talk to him. He is very smart, you know, and he feels things so deeply. I think he is more like a brother to me, though. Or a friend. You can love a friend, no?"

"Oh yes indeed," Ysabella said. "And friends can

become lovers. Some say that is the best way to find real love—though it would never do for me. I want that moment, that instant where your eyes meet his and suddenly, he is all. Even if it ends badly, I want that."

We were quiet then, and I considered what Ysabella had said. No, I didn't feel that moment, that kind of connection, with Owen. He was my dear friend. Maybe that would grow to be something more, and maybe it wouldn't. I wasn't sure if I wanted it to. Love seemed very complicated to me. But I was too tired to worry about it, and the bed was too soft. I was asleep in minutes.

The men with the hoods come back. My dear friend Sigrid sleeps on the mattress beside me, for all her family is gone. The men push their way into the house, and this time Mama is more angry than scared. She tries to make them leave, but they laugh at her. They have been drinking. They stink of it.

"We know there is a witch," the tallest one says. "Our village was untouched until one of your girls came over the mountain to sell her wool. Then everyone fell ill. My wife and son died. My uncle. My two brothers and all their families. It was your witch that put a curse of death on us."

Sigrid and I tremble in the corner. I know who had gone over the mountain with her wool. I know why she had gone: There is no food, no money, nothing. She is starving. We are all beginning to starve. She had done it for us. Sigrid had done it for us.

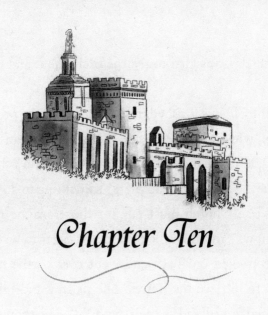

Chapter Ten

DAYS PASSED IN A FLURRY OF EATING, PER-
forming, and deep, dreamless sleeping. I couldn't
remember ever feeling better—full, rested, and, at last,
not fearful. Something in me that had been closed for
a long, long time began to open, just a bit, in the safety
and comfort of the palace. I almost wished we would
never leave.

Owen spoke to the prince-bishop's steward and
learned that the envoy planned to make part of his
journey by ship. "There is a big river running from . . .
I think he said Lyon? It goes all the way to Avignon.
It will be so much faster than going on foot, or even
horseback. And from there it's only two days' ride to

Marseille!" I was glad to see the excitement and relief in his eyes.

Bishop Denis finished his business with the prince-bishop, whatever it was. "He gave Englebert an official papal proclamation, I believe," Raymond told us. "About the Sickness. And there's something to do with taxes. The Church must pay for those ermine robes somehow!" And then the bishop was eager to be off.

We packed our bags and went over to the monastery to retrieve the horses. The palfrey and Johann appeared as well fed as I felt, but Old Man, though he gave us a pleased look when we entered the stable, was breathing heavily just standing still.

"I fear we must leave you behind, old friend," Raymond said to him, stroking his long nose. "We will be traveling with soldiers, and you could never keep the pace."

"Oh no!" Ysabella cried. "We can't leave Old Man!"

Raymond shrugged. "We have to, my dear. It wouldn't be fair to him to force him to trot along with the younger mounts. He'd be in the soup pot before the first day's sunset. And I know that Bernard will treat him well. He has a soft heart for horses."

Ysabella frowned, but she knew he was right. I

looked into Old Man's dark, tranquil eyes. He had such long lashes; how had I not noticed before?

"Goodbye, Old Man," I whispered. "Enjoy the food!"

Owen, listening, laughed. "It's a nice end for a good horse," he said. "Though I hope that sour Brother Marco doesn't try to make him work!"

I blinked back tears. How ridiculous, to cry for a horse. I was sure Raymond would tease me for it, but he just smiled at me and ruffled my hair.

"Onward," he said, and we crossed the busy square to join Bishop Denis's retinue, massed in front of the palace.

There were priests, monks who worked as scribes, soldiers, and servants traveling with the papal envoy. A dozen mules carried everything necessary to ensure that the pope's representative journeyed in comfort. We passed out of the city and moved south, stopping at manor houses and castles and, occasionally, smaller and meaner homes. At those places, it was clear that their hosts were spending every last coin they had on food and entertainment. The envoy seemed to expect such luxury, but I felt guilty taking their food and tried to eat less than I wanted. I knew how hard they'd worked for it and how their generosity now could leave them hungry when winter came.

We musicians rode together, with an extra horse supplied by the bishop for Jacme. We kept to ourselves in the daytime, but in the evenings we took our meals with the soldiers, and Raymond won money from them at dice. We got to know a few of them well: Aymon, whose nostrils flared like a cow's when he lost a bet; Henri, who looked old enough to be a grandfather and had survived the terrible battle at Crécy; Ewart, who had three sweethearts waiting for him in three different towns. Sometimes the scribes would sneak away and join us. One of the scribes took a great liking to Ysabella. He was very young, beardless still. His name was Brother Gille. Ysabella was kind to him for the most part, though occasionally she would tease him for the way he looked at her.

"Are you certain you're a monk?" she would say, and he would blush as red as a sunset from the top of his tonsured head to the neck of his robe.

After the bishop had dined, we often performed for him and his hosts. "Why did I ever agree to this?" Raymond moaned after several days. "I am so sick of holy music! How I long to play a love song, or a heroic ballad at the least!"

Owen laughed. "Are you certain that Bishop Denis would object to a ballad?"

"Oh, just look at him," Raymond said, motioning at the bishop. He rode near the front of the caravan. He seemed to pray continuously, even on horseback. His eyes were ever closed, his hands clasped, his head bent forward.

"I think he is asleep, not praying," Ysabella said, and I giggled.

"At least it's a safe journey," Jacme noted. "And relatively comfortable. We don't have to worry about where to sleep or eat."

"I'd rather starve than play '*Ave Domina*' again," Raymond grumbled.

I didn't mind, though. The meals were good and plentiful, we slept in outbuildings or warm stables, protected from the elements, and the swords at the soldiers' sides gave me an unfamiliar, welcome feeling of safety. Ysabella and I took advantage of the warm, bright days to compose new songs as we rode, and when the bishop and his retinue had retired for the night, we taught the tunes to Raymond, Jacme, and Owen. I was tasked with writing down the words so we would remember them, and my writing improved quickly.

The journey was a constant wonder, a chance to look around and really see the land we passed through. Thick forests, where the soldiers caught and killed a wild boar, which we roasted on a spit that night—the most delicious thing I had ever tasted. Chalk-white cliffs that soared high above the River Meuse. Tiny villages where every last inhabitant ran to the road from the cottages and fields to stare with wonder at the envoy and his red-cloaked, red-hatted companions. Huge hilltop stone castles where lords and ladies welcomed us with grand ceremony and even grander feasts. I felt as if I spent most of the time with my head swiveling left and right to take in the beauty, the grandeur, the *differentness* of it all.

We spent a night at the ancient castle-fortress at Bouillon, where the castellan grudgingly gave us hard beds in chilly rooms. Then, at last, we passed into French lands. The terrain grew less forested and hilly, and the warm sun shone on small fields worked by farmers who gaped at our passing. When the long spring day faded toward evening, we stopped at a stone manor house. Our host, the Count d'Aure, had been warned days before that we were coming, and he met us with several local clerics. By now I was used to the great pomp that announced our entry into each town, with priests and singing and prayers. I wondered that the envoy didn't get tired of it, but he seemed to love holding out his hand and having his ring kissed, sitting in the place of honor, and, most of all, being served the daintiest and tastiest of special foods—quail, venison in verjuice, marzipan tarts—at the nightly feasts.

Stiff as always at the end of a long day riding, I walked a bit to stretch my legs, but I stopped at the sound of a cry from Ysabella.

"Jacme!"

I turned to see Jacme sprawled on the ground. Had his knees buckled as mine almost had when I dismounted? I trotted toward him; Ysabella and Raymond were bent over him as he lay in the long grass. They turned horrified faces to me, and I drew back.

"No," I whispered. I looked down. Jacme wasn't trying to stand up; he was breathing heavily, his brow dotted with sweat. Quickly I knelt, putting a hand to his forehead. It was as hot as a brand. I untied his cloak and pulled it away from his neck. Yes, there it was—the swelling. The cursed, fatal swelling.

Ysabella let out a choked sob, and Raymond reached down to touch Jacme's pale face.

"No!" I said again, sharply. "Don't touch him. Let me do it. I have had the Sickness. I will not get ill."

The others looked at me blankly.

"No one gets it twice. If you live through it, you are safe," I said. I wasn't sure this was true, but I had nursed the sailors on the *Saint Nicholas* and stayed well.

Owen drew in a deep breath. "You have had it? How did you survive?" he asked.

"I don't know. I just did."

"*Mon Dieu*," Raymond whispered.

I looked around. The others had vanished inside the manor house or into the stables. Nobody was watching. "Find a place where no one can see us, and make him a pallet," I ordered. "Bring fresh water. A blanket. Something for him to vomit into. A cloth for his head."

Ysabella stood, ready to do what I asked. "But should we not tell the bishop? He has his own doctor traveling with him!"

"The doctor will bleed him, and that will kill him outright," I said. I had seen it before. Our village's wisewoman, Agneta, had bled Hakon. An hour later, he died. "And if the bishop knows he is sick . . ." My voice trailed off. I wasn't sure what would happen if he knew. He might kill us, to keep the illness from spreading. I had heard of such things as well.

"Can you help him?" Ysabella pleaded. "Can you save him?"

I couldn't meet her eyes. "Bring me what I need. I will do what I can."

Owen and Raymond carried Jacme into a rickety outbuilding near the stables. It was obviously used for storage; scythes and other tools, broken and mended, leaned against the walls. We laid Jacme on a pallet of blankets on the dirt floor, and I pulled another blanket over him. He had begun to shiver violently.

"My head . . . ," he whispered. I nodded. The headache was always unbearable. I took a cloth, dipped it in water, wrung it out, and placed it gently on his brow, dabbing away the sweat. Raymond poked his head into the shed.

"Out," I said firmly.

"I must be with him," Raymond begged. "Don't make me leave him."

"He won't know you are there," I said. "And you will get sick."

Raymond backed away. "I will be close. Please, don't let him die. Please."

I looked at him, then away. I couldn't bear the anguish in his eyes. "It is not in my hands."

Hours passed as slowly as days. Ysabella offered me a bowl of stew, but I couldn't eat. I sponged Jacme when he sweated and covered him when he shivered. For a time his vision cleared, and he spoke to me. His sweet singer's voice was raspy.

"Where is Raymond?"

"Just outside," I said. "I told him to stay out so he wouldn't get sick."

"Good," Jacme whispered. "Thank you." He grasped my hand, but in minutes his grip weakened and his eyes filmed over again. He moaned and vomited, and I cleaned up the bloody bile. Then he fell into a deep sleep. His breathing was even, and his face, contorted from the pain, smoothed. I allowed myself, for a moment, to hope.

Then I rolled up his shirt to bathe his arms and chest, and recoiled. His plague boils and the skin around them had begun to blacken. It had been this way with my family. With my friends. With the sailors. It was always this way.

I pulled open the door. Raymond, Ysabella, and Owen lay rolled in blankets close by. None of them were sleeping. Raymond sprang up when he saw me.

"Is he—" But he couldn't finish.

I shook my head. "You should say goodbye," I told

him. "Do not touch him—if you can help it." I was glad it was dark; I didn't want to see his face.

Raymond went into the hut, and I sat on his blanket roll, facing away from the others. I was numb, stunned. I felt as if I were outside my own body. I pinched my arm, hard, to see if I could bring me back to myself, but I barely felt it. My mind had gone blank again, as it had been on the ship in the early days. Nearly as it had been when Owen and the sailors found me.

Ysabella huddled with Owen, her head on her knees, his arm around her shoulders. When Raymond came out after a long, silent time, she stood and went inside. I could hear her talking to her brother, but I couldn't make out the words. Finally she too stumbled out of the hut. She went to Raymond and threw her arms around him, shaking with sobs.

I got to my feet again. I ached with weariness. "I'll stay with him," I said to Ysabella and Raymond. Raymond nodded, but Ysabella was crying too hard to respond. I wasn't even sure she'd heard.

The air in the hut had grown thick with the peculiar smell the Sickness gave off: metallic blood and the sour odor of the erupting boils, mixed with a strange sweetness on the breath of the dying. When Jacme grew agitated again, I sang my lullaby to him, as I had to the dying Sean on shipboard, and he quieted. When I stopped singing, he clawed at the air restlessly, so I kept on, over and over until I was hoarse.

At some point there was noise outside the hut. Loud voices, Raymond shouting. I heard Ysabella scream. In his delirium, Jacme must have heard it too; he roused and began to moan. I went to the door and flung it open, determined to keep the others quiet. Jacme, like anyone, deserved to die in peace.

Outside I saw three of the bishop's soldiers, swords out. One of them held a torch. Its light cast wild, flickering shadows on Raymond, Ysabella, and Owen, distorting their features.

"You must be quiet!" I hissed. The soldiers backed away from me.

"They want to burn the hut!" Ysabella cried. "They're mad—they want to burn it, with Jacme inside!"

I stared at the soldiers. One of them was the old man, Henri. "He has played cards with you," I said to him. "What if this were your own son?" Henri looked down, but not before I'd seen the fear in his eyes. I turned to the others—Ewart and one with a thick black beard whom I did not know well. "He is still alive," I told them. "If you burn him, it is murder."

"He has the Sickness," the black-bearded soldier protested.

"He does not," I said firmly. "He has the pox. Do you want to see for yourself?" I took a step closer to them, and they backed away still farther, looking uncertain.

"Get you gone," Raymond told them. "If you let us tend our friend in peace, I'll consider your dice debt paid."

The soldiers exchanged glances, then nodded. "Ye'll be dead yourself soon enough anyway, old man," the black-bearded one sneered. Henri cuffed him, but as they started back to the stables where they and the bishop's servants were staying the night, he said to his companions, "Pox, my arse!"

I went back into the hut, where Jacme lay quiet again, and insensible. I took up my song once more. The time between his inhales grew long and longer. After a while, they stopped. I sang on for a little while, and then I stopped too. I pulled Jacme's blanket up over his face. Then, dazed and desolate, I curled up in a corner of the hut and waited for dawn.

I start to feel light-headed in the afternoon. By dark I have forgotten who I am, where I am. I know my mother is tending me. No one else has such soft hands. Then I don't feel her touch on me any longer.

I don't know how much time passes. My sister Gudrun brings me water. I hear her voice whispering to me. I feel the heat of her tears dripping on me. Then I can't sense her anymore. I am so thirsty. I sleep and wake, and when I wake, I wonder: Is everyone gone? Is there anyone left? I decide that if they are all dead, I should die too. My heart obeys me. But I cannot make my body die.

It is dawn. A week later? Two weeks? It has snowed. Everything is white, and strangely silent. Everyone is dead. The cows lying in the snow, rotting. They have died from not being milked.

I walk to the church. It takes a long time. I am so weak. There is an open grave in the churchyard. Full of bodies. I see my mother in it. She clutches my baby brother. Even in death she holds him tight. My neighbors sprawl beside her. My friend Sigrid. Her body is . . . No. On top is the gravedigger. It is clear that he died before he could fill in the hole. The smell is unbearable. The sight is unbearable. I scream until I lose my voice, until I lose my mind.

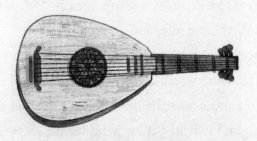

Chapter Eleven

IN THE EARLY MORNING LIGHT, OWEN CAME
into the hut. He put an arm around me and helped me
to stand. Then he found a shovel among the tools and
carried it outside, motioning to me to follow.

"We should bury him," he told the others. Ysabella,
her face swollen from weeping, shook her head.

"We should take him to the church. He must be
buried in consecrated ground," she protested.

"The Count d'Aure told me that there is no room
in the cemetery," Owen said. "He has given permission for us to bury him behind the stables. And he says
the pope has granted remittance of all sins for those
who've died of the Sickness."

Raymond drew in a sharp breath. "Without last rites? Without confession?"

Owen shrugged. "That's what the count says."

"The whole world is in chaos," Raymond whispered. His face was drawn; he looked as if he'd aged decades overnight. He held out his hand for the shovel. "I will do it."

Owen handed him the shovel, and he walked, stoop-shouldered, behind the stable. In a moment we heard the sound of digging.

I looked around me, disoriented after my night in the dark hut. "Where are the others? The horses?" I asked. The stable yard was empty and silent.

"They left before dawn," Owen said. "The news of Jacme's illness spread, and they were afraid."

"They left us?" I was horrified. "Without horses, without food?"

"It could have been worse," Owen told her. "At least they didn't burn down the hut."

"*Hrafnasueltir,*" I muttered.

"What?"

"It means . . . one who starves ravens."

Owen blinked.

"It is a bad word in my language. A soldier who

starves ravens is one who doesn't dare to risk his life in battle. One who doesn't want to fight and die and become raven food."

"A coward?" Owen guessed.

"Yes. A *hrafnasueltir*."

"They were cowards indeed," Ysabella said bitterly. "I wanted to kill that soldier, the one with the black beard."

"So did I," Owen said, shaking his head. "I'm going to help Raymond. Maybe you should . . . ready him?"

I knew what he meant—prepare the body. "I will do it," I said.

"No, I will," Ysabella told me. "He's my brother— my twin. It will be my last . . . my last kindness to him." Her lips trembled.

"I don't think it's safe," I protested. "Please, I don't want you to get sick."

"What do I care if it's safe or not?" Ysabella cried. "Jacme is dead! He's dead! Oh, Jesu, we were together in the womb, Rype! We have been together every day since, every single day. What will I do without him?"

I stepped forward and put my arms around Ysabella. It was the first time I had hugged anyone in as long as I could remember. My arms remembered hugging, though; my body remembered the softness, the warmth of embrace. Holding her like that unraveled me, loosened my hold on myself. I began to cry. I had stopped crying so long ago, even before my family died. There had been too many losses to weep for them all. I'd thought that I had no tears left, that I had used them up. But I was wrong. I sobbed, the tears burning as they ran down my cheeks and soaked my kirtle. And finally, as I clung to her, Ysabella's stiff body relaxed, and she nodded.

"I will watch as you ready him," she said quietly. "I will bear witness for him."

We went into the hut, leaving the door open to dispel the odor. Using a clean cloth and the water that was left after my night of nursing, I bathed Jacme gently, avoiding the blackened boils. His face was nearly untouched by the marks of the Sickness; I was glad for that. Beside me, Ysabella murmured prayers as I wrapped Jacme in a blanket, swaddling him as I once had swaddled my baby brother Per. When I was done, we stood and looked down at him.

"Do you really think all his sins are forgiven?" Ysabella said, low.

"If the pope has said so, it must be true," I assured her, though truly I had no idea. But where else could

Jacme, so graceful and kind and happy, be but in Heaven?

Owen and Raymond came back, the grave dug. Together the four of us carried the body, surprisingly heavy, out of the hut and behind the stables. I could see people watching from the manor house, but nobody attempted to come near.

The grave was neat and deep, near a stately oak tree.

"He will have a lovely view," Ysabella said, her voice cracking. The spot looked over the manor's fields, where grain was beginning to grow high. The sun was warm, and birds called. It should have been cold, bleak, pelting down rain, to match our feelings. But the Sickness had no effect on nature. Life went along as it always had, no matter who died.

Raymond and Owen laid the body beside the hole. They climbed in, reached up, and took Jacme in their arms. Gently, gently they lowered the body until it rested on the bottom. Raymond placed his hand on Jacme's cheek for a moment. Then they climbed out.

We stood over the grave, and Owen intoned the words that I had heard so often, on the *Saint Nicholas* and in Skeviga: "O Lord, grant him eternal rest, and let everlasting light shine upon him." Then I stepped forward. With no instrument accompanying me, I sang the words I had composed during the long night in the hut.

> *"How he moved*
> *Like a willow*
> *So much beauty, so much grace*
> *How he laughed*
> *Always joyful*
> *With a smile that lit his face*
> *How he sang*
> *Like the woodlark*
> *In the morning, with the sun*
> *How we mourn*
> *How we'll miss him*
> *For his time with us is done."*

Raymond took one of my hands, and Ysabella took the other. "Again," Raymond whispered, and I sang the brief, sorrowful melody once more. Then Raymond handed the shovel to Ysabella, and she threw a shovelful of dirt into the grave, wincing at the sound it made as it landed. One by one, we all did the same. Then Owen finished the job.

Sometime during the night, Owen had fashioned a cross out of two sticks, whittled into shape and bound with a length of leather. He pushed it into the mound of dirt that covered Jacme. At last we turned away from the grave and made our way back to the hut.

Outside the ramshackle building, there was a wrapped parcel that hadn't been there before. Ysabella opened it. There were cheeses and dried sausages and two small loaves of bread. Again I looked toward the manor house, but the windows and doorway were empty. Raymond added the parcel to his satchel and hefted it onto his shoulder. Wordlessly, we made our way back to the road and set off. Only Ysabella looked back, silent tears running down her cheeks.

We walked all day, stopping once to eat a few bites of the cheese and sausage. A farmer allowed us to spend the night in his stable. We were exhausted, and though I couldn't imagine sleeping, we all fell asleep moments after we lay down in the scratchy straw and slept without dreams until morning. Days passed in this quiet way. Raymond walked behind us, veering off the road sometimes but always appearing again before we began to worry. Ysabella wept as she walked. Owen and I trudged on stolidly, lost in our own thoughts.

I found some comfort in thinking of Jacme, his joy

as he danced, his love of music and his sister and Raymond. He was a person who brought brightness into the lives of everyone he met. Why were some people like that, I wondered, and others gloomy, or harsh, or even cruel? Surely it wasn't just how they were made. Some part of it must have to do with how they lived. It seemed to me that part of Jacme's happiness was that he was doing what he loved, and doing it with the folk he loved.

And then I thought about whether I could ever be happy in that way. If I went to England to live with Owen and his family, would that bring me joy? I imagined Owen's mother and sister, both with a quick laugh like Owen's, with Owen's kindness, his sturdy reliability. It would be a fine life, a comfortable life. But could I find that brightness in myself if I were to live in a city home, doing endless, repetitive household chores, destined for marriage with an English boy? When I sank too deep into thoughts like that, Owen would distract me with a gentle touch, or his gap-toothed smile, and I would try to shake off my doubts.

I knew that if any of us were to sicken from Jacme's illness, it would show within a seven-night. I watched the others closely for signs, checked my own neck and armpits often. But none of us showed signs of a fever or swellings, and after a week had passed, I relaxed a little.

We moved slowly at first, fearful of overtaking the papal envoy and his people. It became clear after a time that they had taken a different turn in the road at some point, though, and we quickened our pace. Some villages we passed were empty, ravaged by the Sickness. Others seemed to have been passed over, preserved by some stroke of luck. In those places, people were wary of us and kept their distance, but usually they would provide a bed in a stable or outbuilding and a few mouthfuls of food.

We came to a small, pretty city on the banks of a wide river. At an inn within the city gates, Owen asked the name of the place.

"This is Auxonne," the innkeeper told him, placing a line of tankards on a long wooden table and splashing ale from a jug into them.

Owen gave Raymond a questioning look. "So we are in Burgundy?"

Raymond nodded.

"Are we going to see your patron, then?"

"No," Raymond said. "We are already past Dijon. We'll go on to Lyon and see if we can find a ship going south from there." He picked up one of the tankards and downed the ale quickly, motioning to the inn-keeper to fill it again.

"But your aim was to go to Dijon. If we went there, we could get supplies, money—wouldn't the duke help us?"

"He would," Raymond said. "But when we made plans to go there, we were together, and I was happy. I cannot do it—not now. I will go with Ysabella to Le Puy."

We were together. I knew he was referring to Jacme. I could understand the need to keep away from a place of happy plans or memories. Seeing the place again would pierce like an arrow.

That night, we performed for the first time since Jacme's death. It was awful at the beginning. Our tim-ing was bad; our singing off-key. Ysabella wept through the first two songs, and the audience, most in their cups from the innkeeper's generous pours, tried to jeer us out of the room, hammering their tankards on the table and shouting insults. But it was this that finally roused Raymond from his melancholy. He strummed his lute hard and began to pluck out the tune to "Sing Hey!" the sailors' song Owen had taught him that always brought a drunken audience to their feet. He, Ysabella, and I began to sing, and by the end of the first verse, the men were pounding the table with their fists rather than their mugs, keeping time and singing along with the chorus. At the end of it, Raymond looked drained, but he was smiling, and he took the stew the innkeeper offered us and ate with an appetite I hadn't seen in him since Jacme's death. Even Ysabella looked a little brighter.

"The music is medicine," I whispered to Owen. He nodded.

"Not just for us—for them all," he said, motioning to the men at the tables. The crowd had seemed rough and surly when we started, but now they were talking and laughing. The innkeeper, pleased, offered us a room for the night and asked us to stay on.

"You could bring in a crowd if you played every night," he noted. "Good business for everyone!"

"We're bound for Lyon," Raymond told him. "And onward from there."

"Your loss then—and mine!" the innkeeper said cheerfully, pouring Raymond another mug of ale.

We entered Lyon a few days later, descending to the city from a hilltop that gave us a fine view of the cathedral spires and the two rivers that made the port so busy and vital.

"If we are lucky," Raymond said, "we will find a river ship that will take us all the way south. Then we will be very close to Marseille, and a journey home for you, my friend!" He clapped Owen on the back hard enough to make him stagger.

"It's hard to believe," Owen said. "I can't even imagine being home. It's been so long! My mother must think I've died—if she lives herself." He gave his head a little shake, as if to banish the thought. "And I'll have to tell her . . ." He trailed off.

"Bad news is expected these days," Raymond said gently. "It is the good news—that you are still alive, and home—that will matter most. Imagine her joy, not her sorrow."

Owen managed a smile. "And I will be bringing her a daughter, won't I, Rype?"

I smiled back and nodded. But the idea of England, of being Owen's sister, had grown a little less certain in my mind. I had no clear plan to take its place, though, so I said nothing.

Lyon was a shock of sights, sounds, and smells. It was much more crowded than Liège had been. Streets were lined with shops—bakers, cobblers, tanneries. I reeled at the reek from the fishmonger's, the flash of heat and thunderous noise of hammer on anvil from the blacksmith's. The shouts of the street vendors selling meat pies and rabbit skins and lengths of linen.

The press of bodies in the narrow streets, the odors of bread and spices and horse dung, the clamor of church bells—it was frightening, exhilarating, overwhelming. I was torn between the impulse to crouch against a wall and cover my ears and the longing to open my arms and all my senses to the assault.

Ysabella noticed my flustered expression and took my hand. "It's a wild place," she said. "But as long as we stay together, we will be safe." We pushed through the crowds that jostled and sometimes elbowed us out of the way. At one shop, Ysabella stopped to look at a length of cloth displayed on a wooden shelf that jutted out from the building.

"Oh," she breathed. "Isn't it beautiful? Wouldn't Jacme have loved a cloak made of that?" It was a fine scarlet-red wool, the color of the ripest summer tomato.

The mercer looked at Ysabella appraisingly. "It would cost more than your husband could probably make in a year," he said, and Ysabella laughed.

"If I had a husband, I'm sure that would be true," she acknowledged, and I pulled her away from the mercer's shop. But in our momentary pause, Owen and Raymond had continued on, and the crowd had closed around them and swallowed them up. I stood on tiptoe, hoping to see Owen's green hood above the throng. But there was no sign of him.

"Oh no," I said, turning to Ysabella. "Where are they?" I could tell that my voice was unnaturally high.

Heads turned to look at us, and Ysabella hushed me. "We'll find them. They are heading toward the river, to find a ship. We'll go in that direction." She stopped a woman to ask the way to the river, but the woman glanced at her and passed on, giving her as wide a berth as she could in the mass of people. I knew the look: It was fear of the stranger, for a stranger was as like as not to carry the Sickness.

Finally an older man pointed us in the right direction. "What if they've gone back to look for us?" I panted as we trotted through the narrow streets and passageways. "We'll never find them!"

I saw signs of the Sickness as we hurried along—the marks on doors that showed where the dead lay to be picked up by the body collectors for burial; victims huddled in doorways, hoods pulled low to hide their symptoms. In one alleyway, Ysabella and I stared in horror as two starving dogs, their ribs showing clearly, clawed and growled over a corpse left to rot against a crumbling wall. We backed away, but the scent of food in Ysabella's satchel attracted the dogs, and they followed us as we made our way back to the main street.

For a moment we stood still in the street, trying to decide which way to go. Before Ysabella could ask for directions again, though, a boy of about ten years pointed at us and cried out, "Look! Look at that dog!"

I looked down. One of the dogs was staggering at my feet. As I gazed at it in alarm, it clamped its teeth down on its own tail, moved in a lurching circle, tripped, and fell. It let out a howl that made the foot traffic on the street halt. Its head hit the dirt, and the light left its eyes. Just like that, it was dead. Ysabella and I backed away. The other dog swayed, trying to follow us. It collapsed briefly, then staggered to its feet and ran off, stumbling as it reeled away.

"Witches! They are witches!" the boy shouted. "Look how they have given the Sickness to the dogs! They just touched them, and the dogs died! Catch them, they're witches!"

We don't realize at first that the Sickness isn't just killing people. I see rabbits and mice dead on the ground. Our chickens die. Sigrid's family has a goat, and it dies. The dogs that roam the village disappear. We assume they too are dead. The Haugness family owns two sheep. They are probably the most valuable things in the whole village. When the sheep die, they mourn as if they were family members. At some point, people realize that these animals have the Sickness. They stop feeding them, afraid to go near them. The rest die of starvation.

Chapter Twelve

THE CRY OF "WITCH!" SPREAD FASTER THAN the Sickness ever could. Ysabella was so shocked she couldn't move, but I had heard that word before. I knew what it meant. I grabbed Ysabella's hand and yanked her forward, trying to press through the crowd. We were too slow. Hands grasped at us, pulling our hair and ripping our clothing. I feared that we would be torn to pieces, but it was only moments before soldiers made their way through the maddened throng.

They pulled us away, shouting, "Leave them! Leave them to us!" The mob snarled and protested, but the soldiers dragged us down an alleyway too narrow for a large group to follow. Through street and passageway we rushed, almost yanked off our feet, until we reached a low stone building in a dark alley. A guard stood in front of the door.

"Witches," one of the soldiers said to the guard, and he stepped back, uneasy.

"I don't want those type in my gaol," he protested. "They'll do something to me, something wicked. Throw them in the river!"

"That's not our job," the other soldier said, gripping my arm so tightly I had to bite my lip to keep from crying out. "They stay here till the judge tries 'em. Then they burn."

The soldiers pulled us into the building. There was a narrow corridor, and off it was a series of thick wooden doors. We could hear cries from inside the cells. The guard opened one door, and the soldiers thrust us inside.

"No magicking, you witches," the guard warned us. "I'll run you through, trial or no!" He brandished his lance, and we shrank back into the room as the guard slammed the door. We could hear the latch descend. Then we were alone.

It had all happened so quickly that I'd barely had time to react. But now, trapped in the tiny, chill stone room, I began to shiver. This was too familiar. I pulled on my braid, stood on one foot, tried to breathe slowly. I didn't want to shut down, to stop thinking. I needed to think.

Ysabella stood wide-eyed and stunned. "What—" she began, but she couldn't finish.

"They think we're witches," I whispered, lowering my foot. "Witches causing the Sickness. They'll burn us, like they did to Sigrid."

"Oh Jesu," Ysabella moaned. She sank to the floor, which was damp and smelly and strewn with straw. There was nothing in the cell but a narrow pallet and a chamber pot. A barred window, so high up on the wall that we couldn't look out, let in just enough light for us to see each other's frightened faces. I began to pace around the room. Three paces across, five from end to end. Three across, five down. Three across, five down. Moving made me stop shaking.

"What will happen to us?" Ysabella murmured. She didn't seem to expect an answer, and I didn't offer one. The people in the other cells had quieted, and the only sound was my footsteps as I walked the boundaries of the cell.

"What did you mean, 'like they did to Sigrid'?" Ysabella said after a time. She sounded calmer.

I grimaced. "She . . . she was my friend. Back in Skeviga."

"Sit," Ysabella said, patting the pallet. "Tell me. You promised me you would tell your story, all those weeks ago."

All those weeks ago—when Jacme was alive. I ignored her and kept pacing.

"Please. I'm afraid, Rype. Talk to me."

I stopped and looked at her. My tale wouldn't ease her fear, I knew that. But I had promised—and perhaps it was better that Ysabella knew.

I sat on the damp pallet, took a deep breath, and began.

"My village was very small, on the sea. Everyone knew everyone. My father was a fisherman. Most of the men were. I had a sister, Gudrun, and a brother, Per. He was just a baby." I stopped. It hurt deep in the pit of my stomach to tell. I could see Skeviga in my mind's eye, the little wooden cottages, the green garden patches, the dark sea just below.

"Go on."

"My grandmother was the first to get sick in Skeviga. We'd heard about the Sickness, of course. It was in the next village. Many were sick there. Mormor died very quickly. She was old and had been ill the winter before. She wasn't strong."

Ysabella patted my hand. I stared down at the floor. A beetle lay on its back in the straw, its legs kicking.

"It seemed like everyone in the village got ill after that. They died and died. Papa died, and all the other fishermen. We had funerals at first, but there were so many . . . The priest said it was our fault, for being sinful." I took a deep breath. "Then the men came from over the mountain. Most in their village were dead. They said it was witchcraft that had spread the Sickness—that someone had poisoned their wells. My best friend Sigrid had gone to their village to try to get food. Without the fishermen, we were starving. They claimed Sigrid was the witch."

Ysabella drew in a sharp breath.

"They took her and beat her. She got away from them and came back to us, but they came and got her again. They tied her and built a pyre." I stopped, swallowed hard. Ysabella squeezed my hand. The beetle righted itself and scurried across the room.

"You don't have to—"

"No, I do. I want to. I have to. They . . . they burned her in front of the church. Mama didn't want me to watch, but I did. She was my friend. I tried to keep my eyes on hers while she burned so she would know she wasn't alone, that I was praying for her. She suffered unbearably."

"Oh, Rype," Ysabella whispered.

"A little later," I continued, my voice wavering, "the priest died. I was glad of it. He was a liar. Sigrid had never sinned a day in her life." Ysabella nodded. "Then I got sick. I was afraid—I knew I would die. I knew it! Everybody died. But I lived. I didn't know why. I still don't know why. But when I could get up again, and see, and think, everyone was gone. Mama and Per, Gudrun, who had nursed me. Everyone in the village. I saw them all in the churchyard, lying in the grave we had dug for ourselves. I was the only one left."

Ysabella was silent.

"After that, I . . . I don't really know what happened. The next thing I remember is Owen, and his father, and the other sailors, and going on his ship. And then we met you."

Ysabella squeezed my hand again.

"I'm so sorry, Rype," she said. Her voice was thick with tears.

"It isn't an unusual story," I said matter-of-factly. "I think many people have a story like that."

"Everybody has a story by now, I suppose," Ysabella said. "But yours is yours alone, and so dreadful. Thank you for telling it to me. I'm glad to know it."

I had thought that telling what had happened would make me weep, or at the very least trap me in the terrible memories I'd worked so hard to bury. But it did not. Instead, I felt lighter, as if the words I'd spoken had weight, and I had laid them down. I could almost remember what it felt like to be my old self, a village girl just concerned with salting fish and weaving wool, whose only knowledge of death was the accidental drowning of an uncle or the gentle passing of an aged village elder.

It was dark in the cell now. Night had fallen outside. Ysabella pulled a hunk of bread from her satchel, and we shared it. Nobody came with food or water. Nobody came at all. We curled up on the pallet and tried to sleep, though the cries that sounded occasionally from the other cells wove their way into my dreams and turned them to restless nightmares.

In the morning, my mouth was as dry as old leather. When the cell door finally opened, a different guard stood there holding a mug. I reached out, but he held it away from me.

"Are you truly witches?" he asked, his eyes narrow.

"No, of course not," Ysabella told him. "We are singers—troubairitz. We write songs and sing them."

"Songs?" He seemed confused by the idea. "Well, are you Jews?"

"We're Christians, like you," Ysabella said. "Why do you ask that?"

He raised an eyebrow. "It might go better for you if you were Jews. The pope has sent his man here to say that Jews are not to be blamed for the Sickness. But he hasn't said the same of witches!"

"We are neither," Ysabella said. "Just singers, nothing more."

"The pope's man?" I said. "Do you mean the envoy? The one with the funny hat?"

"A strange flat hat he has. He's with the archbishop now, to give him the decree."

"The decree?"

"The archbishop read it out to the people in town. I wasn't there, but my girl was. She told me it says we cannot blame the Jews for the Sickness anymore. So I've had to release the ones we had here."

"The envoy is still here, in Lyon? With all his people?" I asked. An idea was growing in my mind. I glanced at Ysabella, and she raised an eyebrow at me.

"He's got dozens of priests with him," the guard

said. "We're overrun by 'em!" Finally he gave the mug to me, and I drank. It was sour ale, but at least it wet my mouth. I gave half to Ysabella.

"Do you think . . . could we write a letter to someone? Is that allowed?" Ysabella made her voice gentle, pleading.

"You can write?"

Ysabella nodded. The guard thought about it. He was a young man, with smooth cheeks and brown wavy hair under his helmet. He didn't look cruel, as the other guard had.

"Maybe if I can find a quill and something to write on . . . ," the guard mused. "But what do I get in return?"

Ysabella and I exchanged another look.

"Well," I said, "you said you had a girl. Do you plan to wed?"

"If she'll have me," the guard said. "But there's another man, a cooper—she likes him well enough. And his pay is better."

I nodded thoughtfully. "But she might like you better if you gave her something of great value."

"You have something of value? Give it over, then." The guard stepped closer, and I backed away.

"I mean a song."

The guard's face fell. "A song? That's not a thing. It's a . . . a song! How would that help me?"

With her most bewitching smile, Ysabella broke in. "Oh, sir, a song is something all ladies love! A romantic song, a song that tells how you adore her—how could she resist? No one can resist a love song."

The guard mulled this over. "Is that truly so?" he demanded.

"Indeed it is," Ysabella assured him, her tone sweet and musical. "It's how my own husband won me. I loved another, a handsomer man, a richer man, but then I met my husband, and he sang to me of his love. It was the most delightful song I had ever heard. And then I could see nothing but him." I kept my face blank. How skillfully Ysabella lied!

"And where is he now?" the guard asked, suspicious. "Why has he left you to burn or rot in prison?"

"He is dead, sir, with so many others. But I mourn him every day." Ysabella bent her head, and a tear dropped on the straw. I forced my own expression into one of sorrow.

"A song," the guard said thoughtfully. "I suppose it is worth a try. I will find you something to write with, and when I come back, you will have a song for me."

"What is your name, sir?" Ysabella asked. "And your lady's?"

"I am Jehan, and she is called Isabeau."

"Why, that is almost the same as my name!" Ysabella said. "How wonderful!"

The guard smiled. "She is almost as pretty as you," he said. "I will be back as soon as I can."

"Bring us something to eat!" Ysabella called as he pulled the heavy door closed behind him.

As soon as he was gone, I turned to her. "Who are you writing?" I asked.

"Do you remember the envoy's scribe? Brother Gille?"

"The blushing monk? Of course, I remember. But—" Suddenly I understood. "Ah. I see what you are planning! They are all at the archbishop's palace. You will write to him and tell him what has happened to us. A good thought!"

Ysabella was pleased. "And your idea of paying with a song was good as well."

"Brother Gille was daft for you," I said. "I'm sure he would try to get us released. Though I don't know if he has any say in such things."

"He was smart," Ysabella mused. "Barely out of his

swaddling clothes, but smart. If anyone could find a way . . ."

We worked on the song as we waited for the guard's return. It was much harder, I found, to compose a song when we only had a little time. But at last we had a verse we both liked:

"Fair Isabeau, benevolent and gentle—
She is the prize I've longed for all my life.
And if she were to say she did not want me
I'd seek no other lady for my wife.
For she is lovely, sweet, and most appealing;
Her skin is soft, her eyes are deepest blue
And when she smiles, the sun itself is challenged
But when she frowns, the sun is gone from view.
Oh, be my love, my Isabeau, my darling!
Be mine, my sweet, my heart, my dearest friend.
If you say yes, my joy will be eternal—
If you say no, I know my life will end."

"What if her eyes are brown?" I asked, and Ysabella smiled.

"I have a line to substitute if they are," she said. "If they are green, though, we're in trouble!"

I snorted, holding back my laugh. I had a feeling that the prison hadn't often heard laughter. And the idea of laughing when we faced the penalty for witchcraft . . . but I realized, with a shock, that I wasn't nearly as afraid as I had been. Was it just that Ysabella was with me? Or had telling my friend what happened to Sigrid cast out the fear?

It wasn't long after that when Jehan reappeared. "I have what you need," he said. "But first, the song."

"What color are Isabeau's eyes?" I asked.

"Blue. No, more than blue. The color of the midday sky in autumn," Jehan replied. His voice was dreamy.

"Why, you are a poet yourself!" Ysabella said, bestowing one of her more charming smiles on him. He looked down at the floor, embarrassed.

Together, we sang the song we'd composed, to the tune of "Great Joy from Loving Well." Our voices blended well. By the time we were finished, tears stood in Jehan's eyes. He turned away, wiping them furtively.

"It is called 'Fair Isabeau,'" Ysabella said. "Do you think she will like it?"

"She . . . she may," Jehan replied, trying to sound offhand. "But how will I give it to her? I can neither read nor write. Nor can she."

"We will teach you to sing it," I suggested. "Can you sing?"

"A bit," Jehan said. "In the tavern, you know—when everyone's singing."

"It will mean all the more if you sing it," I said, and Ysabella nodded. "She will hear the sincerity in your voice, even if you miss a note or two."

"Let me write my message first," Ysabella said. "If you will take it to the archbishop's palace and give it into the hand of the scribe Gille, we will teach you until you can sing 'Fair Isabeau' perfectly."

"Well, hurry then!" Jehan commanded. He went to the cell door and peered down the corridor in each direction, making sure no other guards were near. Then, from under his tunic, he handed Ysabella the writing tools.

"What is the name of this place?" Ysabella asked.

"Saint Georges Gaol."

Quickly Ysabella scratched out a note to Brother Gille and signed it. She showed it to me when she was done. Slowly, I made out the words.

We are prisoners in Saint Georges Gaol.
We are accused of witchcraft and will
be tried. We face certain death without
your aid. We beg of you: Please send
help!

"Will he act?" I asked.

"We can only hope," Ysabella said. She turned to Jehan. "Do you know when we are to be tried?"

"I shouldn't worry about that," Jehan said. "They prefer to keep the prisoners here until they die more naturally. A trial is costly, and the judge is lazy."

"What do they die of?" I asked.

"Oh, the bloody flux. Or starvation. Some of them are tortured. It depends." Jehan noted the alarm in my eyes and hurried to reassure us. "I'll make sure you have food enough, don't worry. I'll bring you something as soon as I find someone to deliver your note."

"Please, can you not deliver it yourself?" Ysabella begged. "It is less likely to fall into the wrong hands—I know we can trust you." She gave him a beseeching look.

"I'll have to find someone to replace me here," Jehan said. "It may take a while. If they grow suspicious—well, it could be worth my post at least. And at worst . . ."

"I feel sure you can do it," Ysabella said. Her voice trembled slightly.

Jehan set his jaw and nodded. "I'll return when I can, and then you must teach me my song." He took the note and hurried out, locking the heavy door behind him.

Ysabella sighed, sitting back on the pallet. "I thought perhaps he would leave the door unlocked— 'accidentally,'" she said.

"Then he'd be sure to be caught and punished— and for two girls he doesn't know," I pointed out.

Ysabella got up again and began to pace. "I never realized that gaol was so dull," she said. "Jesu, what do people do who are locked in here for months—or years?"

"We can sing," I suggested. "Or compose."

"It was hard enough to write Jehan's song in this place. I cannot compose something worthwhile here, with these terrible smells. I like to work in the open air. I have to be able to *breathe*."

I sighed. Sometimes, Ysabella sounded a little like a spoiled child.

"Then let's just sing." I started a love song from the North, and reluctantly Ysabella joined in. As time passed, moving the shadows from the window along the wall, we sang, and when we stopped to catch our breaths, a cry went up from the other cells.

"More! Go on!" they called. So we sang songs of adventure, and songs of ancient kings and voyagers, and heroic ballads that elicited cheers from the prisoners. By the time Jehan came back, we were hoarse.

"Did you find him?" Ysabella demanded. "Did you give him the note?"

"It wasn't easy," Jehan said. "They didn't want to let me in at all. I had to wait for a long time. But I've never been in the archbishop's palace before—what a place! Everything gold, and naked paintings of angels everywhere! It doesn't seem right for a religious man." I hid a smile.

"He came out to me after a time, your Brother Gille. Seems a nice enough fellow, for a monk. So I gave him the note, and he read it and went a little pale. Then he rushed off, but he had a manservant give me a coin. So it wasn't time wasted!"

"Good, that's very good," Ysabella said. She looked much calmer. I hadn't realized how frightened she was.

"Now, teach me the song," Jehan demanded.

"Yes, of course. Only—could we have something to eat and drink first?"

Jehan brought us some bread and cheese and ale, not sour this time. "This is from my own supper," he told us, and he scuffed his boot on the ground when Ysabella placed a grateful hand on his arm.

"You are very kind to us," she said. We ate quickly, then instructed Jehan to take off his helmet while we taught him "Fair Isabeau." He had a nice voice, undistinguished but clear and steady, and he learned quickly. By the time darkness fell in our little cell, he knew the words by heart.

"The watch will be changing," he said. "You'll have a new guard for the evening. I have to go."

"That other guard . . . ," Ysabella said hesitantly. "He frightened us."

"He's a brute," Jehan said cheerfully. "But he's more scared of you two than you are of him. He believes you are witches. Here, I'll leave you a torch so you don't have to sit in darkness. And I will be back tomorrow!" He brought a torch from the outer hall and put it in the holder on our wall. Then he was gone, and we were alone once more.

We tried to sleep on the hard, smelly pallet, twisting and turning in discomfort. I had only just managed to doze off when a shouting in the outer hall shocked me wide awake.

"Bring us the witches!" a man's voice called. "We are taking them now. Where are they?"

My heart leaped, and I turned to look at Ysabella. In the guttering light from the torch, I could see my friend's terrified expression, and I knew mine mirrored it. I had been wrong to be unafraid. We would be taken, and tried, and burned alive—just like Sigrid.

After they take Sigrid from our house, I don't see her for three days. I don't know where they keep her. At last they bring her out on a cart pulled by a donkey. She is wild-eyed and wild-haired. There is a bruise purpling her cheekbone and her left arm dangles uselessly. She looks as if she hadn't slept at all, or eaten.

I hadn't known there were so many folk left in Skeviga— I'd thought most of them had died. But perhaps some have come over the mountain to watch. People love to see others get punished. Only, this is Sigrid.

Mama clasps my hand. "Come away, daughter," she whispers. "There is nothing you can do for her. You do not need to watch this."

But she is wrong. I do need to watch. I need to bear witness for Sigrid. It is what I can do for her. It is all I can do.

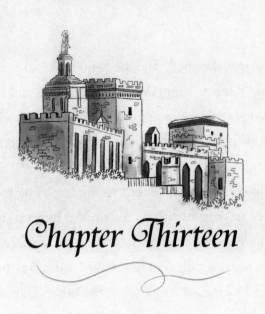

Chapter Thirteen

THE HORRID GUARD UNLOCKED THE DOOR, and soldiers rushed inside. They grabbed Ysabella and me, lifted us bodily off the floor, carried us from the cell and down the hall and out and away from the prison. The fear was so strong in me that I couldn't move or speak. I hung as limp as a slaughtered sheep over the shoulder of the man who bore me, the metal of his armor digging into my ribs.

The fresh air outside roused me a bit, but it wasn't until we were moving swiftly through the narrow streets that I began to struggle. Immediately the soldier carrying me placed me on my feet. He raised his helmet.

My jaw dropped, and he winked at me. It was Owen. "Keep moving, Witch!" he growled, and I scurried along with the rest of them. Ysabella too had been released from the soldiers' clutches, and she grabbed my hand.

"How—" she started, but we were moving too fast for her to have breath to finish. We hurried up and down streets and alleyways and finally emerged in a square with a tall, square-towered cathedral on one end and a long, squat palace at the other. The soldiers guided us around the back of the palace, which stood alongside a rushing river. There was a small wooden door set into the palace wall. A soldier knocked on it, and it was flung open by Raymond.

"Well, *grâce à Dieu*—thank God!" he said, hugging first Ysabella, then me. "You two know how to have an adventure, do you not? In gaol, no less! Now I am no longer the only one of us who has languished in a gaol cell."

I stared at him and burst out laughing. "Of course, you have been in gaol," I managed at last, wiping away tears. "I won't even ask for what!"

"Oh, rest assured I will tell you regardless," Raymond said.

I looked at the soldiers ringing us. They were the

same men whom Raymond had beaten at dice evening after evening, the same who had threatened to burn down the hut where Jacme lay dying and who had left us in the middle of the night. I didn't know whether to thank them or curse them.

Ysabella stepped forward. "You have redeemed yourselves," she said to the oldest of them, Henri. "We are grateful for the rescue, and we forgive you for abandoning us."

"You had the Sickness!" the black-bearded soldier protested, but the one I recalled was named Ewart cuffed him on the helmet and said, "We are glad to atone, Mistress. It was shameful what we did, but it was at Bishop Denis's command, and we are his men."

"I understand," Ysabella said graciously. Then she noticed Brother Gille standing behind the soldiers. "Brother Gille!" she cried. "Was this your doing? Have I you to thank for our rescue?"

Brother Gille blushed red from the top of his tonsured head down. "I . . . I only told Master Raymond. He took care of the rest."

Ysabella went to Brother Gille and took his hands in hers. "It could not have been done without your help. We are so grateful."

I managed not to laugh as Brother Gille twitched

and flushed a still deeper shade. I feared he might faint altogether, but Ewart slapped him on the back and said, "Sometimes a monk comes in handy, eh, Mistress?" Then everyone laughed, and Brother Gille yanked his hands from Ysabella's as if he'd been burned and scurried off down the hall.

"The bishop and archbishop know nothing of this," Raymond warned as he led us through the warren of passageways, Owen clanking in his armor behind us.

I looked back at Owen and said, "So you are now a soldier? Have you given up the merchant trade for war?"

Owen laughed. "I begged them to let me go along. I'd always wondered what it was like to wear armor, and now I know. Uncomfortable, is what it's like! It rubs where you don't want to be rubbed and makes an ungodly noise. You can hardly breathe in that helmet. I can't imagine how they march miles in it."

"I'm so glad you came," I said. "We thought—we thought they were taking us to be tried, until I saw your face."

"I'm sorry," Owen said. "There was no way to let you know in advance. We would have warned you if we could! But whatever happened? You were there in the street, and the next minute you were gone—and then it was more than a day before we heard you were imprisoned. We looked everywhere for you!"

I explained the sick dogs, and the mob, and the terrible gaol, and the help of the guard Jehan. Raymond loved the story. "You traded a song for your release! Oh, that will become a legend with the troubadours, if I have anything to say about it!"

We stopped at a bedchamber, and Owen pointed inside. "You can stay here. The bishop doesn't seem to mind that we are back, so I doubt that he'll object to you two."

"He is a very busy man," Raymond said disdainfully. "With all those prayers to say, how could he have the time to make trouble for lowly troubadours?"

"How did you end up here?" Ysabella asked.

"We ran into Brother Gille outside the palace. It was clear that we were not infected, so he invited us in. He was desperately worried about you, Ysabella. You have a conquest in him!"

"Perhaps he isn't meant to be a monk," Ysabella observed, and Raymond laughed.

"God is surely testing him," he said. "Get some sleep, you two. We depart tomorrow, down the river!"

There was a large barrel in the middle of the bed-chamber, and steam rose from the top of it. "What is that?" I asked, pointing.

"It is to bathe in," Raymond said. "Have you never seen a bath before?"

"A bath?" I said, approaching the barrel. "We bathed in the pond, in warm weather. Is this water heated?"

"It is," Raymond said. "And may I be rude enough to say that you need it? I get the impression that your prison was not exactly clean."

I knew he was right. We were streaked with dirt from the damp, muddy gaol floor, and I could smell myself, rank from the rotting straw and the pallet that had been used for years by other prisoners.

When Raymond and Owen had gone, Ysabella and I stripped and stepped into the barrel. The water was perfumed with herbs, and the bath was lined with soft cloths. A small white block lay on a stool nearby. Ysabella picked it up and sniffed it.

"Soap!" she said. "And fine soap at that. The archbishop of Lyon lives well!" She scrubbed herself from head to toe and then passed the bar to me. It smelled like flowers. I followed her lead and washed myself. The warm water, the perfume of the soap, the softness of my own skin as the soap cleansed it—it was one of the most marvelous experiences I'd ever had.

"Have you had a bath like this before?" I asked.

"Oh yes," Ysabella said. "But only in a bathhouse, not at home."

"A whole house for baths?"

Ysabella laughed. "That's right. People go there to bathe and talk, and even eat. It's lovely. Though the soap is nothing like this—it's made of mutton fat." She wrinkled her nose.

I shook my head, spraying Ysabella with water. Baths. Flower soap. What a world I lived in!

In the morning, we rose early and met the others in the palace courtyard. The bishop was there, looking just as plump and prayerful as when we'd last seen him. He took a very formal leave of the archbishop, and then the entourage started out through the iron palace gates.

When we got to the river, we crossed a bridge and kept walking. "Where are we going?" I asked Owen.

"There are two rivers here," he said. "This one is smaller—the Saône. The other one, the Rhône, goes all the way to Avignon, where the pope is, and then to the sea. That is the one we will travel."

"We're going by water?" Raymond had said something to that effect, but I hadn't paid it much mind.

"Yes—faster and easier, by far. And probably safer and more comfortable, in Bishop Denis's company. We'll make up some of the time we've lost along the way."

I nodded. The river we were crossing seemed very wide indeed, but when we walked a little farther and arrived at the second river, I was amazed to find it was far broader. I could see where the two waterways came together, at the end of the spit of land we were walking across. Little waves sprang up at the meeting point of the currents, almost like the ocean.

A ship waited for us at the end of a long pier. "That's the *Saintespirit*," Raymond told us.

Owen looked it over with a practiced eye. "It's a *usciere*," he pointed out. "I've seen them in Gravesend. Watch this."

The soldiers dismounted and led their horses to the ship. As I looked on wide-eyed, sailors pulled open a wide door in the hull and laid down planks, and the horses walked uneasily, urged by the sailors, up the planks and into the belly of the ship.

"How strange," Ysabella said. "I have never seen a horse on a ship before!"

"When England goes to war, the soldiers bring their horses on these ships," Owen said. "After all, you can't expect a lord to fight on foot like a commoner!"

We boarded after the bishop's entourage, and the ship's sails went up. In the strong breeze the ship moved quickly downstream. I stood at the railing, breathing in the fresh air, glad to be away from Lyon.

The days on the river passed peaceably. We sailed past villages and vineyards, towns and lone farms. Often people would come to the shore to wave, and I waved back, delighted by their different sizes and shapes, dress and demeanors. It was a strange and pleasing way to travel, away from all the hardship of walking or riding, yet still able to see so much.

When Bishop Denis heard we were aboard, he called for us to perform in the evenings. "More holy tunes!" Raymond grumbled, but we enjoyed the days spent setting sacred texts to music and evenings performing the new songs. After the bishop retired to his quarters belowdecks, we sang love songs and epics to the soldiers and servants.

We were not far from Avignon when I was awakened in the cabin I shared with Ysabella by the ship's sudden shuddering. A cup that stood on a table in the cabin fell over, spilling its remnants of cider.

"What was that?" I whispered, shaking Ysabella.

Ysabella opened her bleary eyes. "What? I didn't hear anything."

"No, it's not a sound. It's the ship—it has stopped. What has happened?"

Ysabella listened. There was shouting from above, and the ship creaked and moaned like a living creature.

"Come," she said, climbing out of bed and pulling her kirtle over her head. I did the same. We clambered up the ladder onto the deck, where day had already broken.

The crew and many of the bishop's men stood motionless at the railing. The sounds of shouting I had heard from below were stilled now. Everyone was silent. Ysabella and I made our way to the starboard side and looked down at the river.

"Jesu," Ysabella whispered. She clutched at my arm.

For a moment I wasn't sure what I was seeing. It looked like piles of logs, twisting and turning in the current. But then I realized: The logs had faces, had arms and legs.

The logs were bodies.

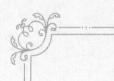

People are not really afraid of death. That is what I learn over the months of suffering. They do not fear the ending. They fear the pain. The pain of the Sickness is immeasurable. And the anguish of their deaths is even worse for the living. There is no way to grieve our way to eventual comfort. There are too many deaths. Before, each one was unique. A drowning, an accident, a slow fading as the months of illness or old age pass—we could mourn and remember and recover. But this—a brother, a sister, an aunt, a father, all in the same day or week—how could anyone recover? So much loss, so much sorrow. So much death. It leaves us numb, unfeeling, and that is worse than the pain.

Chapter Fourteen

I COULD NOT PULL MY EYES AWAY FROM the river's horror. The ship was jammed among dozens and dozens of plague-ridden bodies that were floating down the Rhône, pieces of human flotsam, swollen and discolored and dead. Beside me, Ysabella swayed, and one of the sailors propped her up. I knew Owen had come up behind me from the touch of his hand on my shoulder, but I couldn't turn away. The bodies below were caught in a sharp bend in the river, piling up on one another in the slow current. A dreadful stench rose up from the water, unlike anything I had ever smelled before.

"Make way for the bishop!" a soldier said. Owen

pulled me from the railing as the bishop pushed through the crowd. He looked down, and I heard him gulp and cough. When he turned back, his round face was ashen.

"His Holiness Pope Clement has declared the river a consecrated burial site," he said, his high voice thin and reedy. "There have been so many deaths that the graveyards are filled. He gave permission for the dead to be given sanctified water burial in the Rhône. But—but I believe he did not think there would be so many . . . so many bodies." Like Ysabella, he wobbled on his feet. A soldier approached, but the bishop waved the man away. He took a deep breath and coughed again.

"The shipmaster tells me it may be some time before we can proceed. The *Saintespirit* has to . . . make its way through. It is best that you remain belowdecks unless you are needed above."

A crashing noise came from below my feet. It sounded again and again, like an enormous hammer pounding on the ship's belly. Dazed by what I had seen in the river, I could make no sense of the sound, until a soldier cried, "The horses—they're kicking!"

I turned a questioning face to Owen. He looked bewildered, but then I saw understanding dawn. "The horses smell death. They're afraid. It is maddening them."

"*Mon Dieu,*" Raymond murmured, on Owen's other side. I hadn't even noticed that he'd joined us.

The horse marshal rushed down the ladder with several of his men. But the pounding continued, now mixed with wild braying from the frantic animals. All at once the ship lurched to the starboard side.

"What—" I cried as I began to slide back toward the railing. Owen grabbed me, but he was sliding too.

"To the port side!" one of the sailors called. "The horses have breached the hull! The ship is taking on water!"

The soldiers and sailors and monks scrambled across the deck, trying to even out the distribution of weight so the damaged ship could right itself. But the *Saintespirit* was listing heavily now, and the deck was slick. We slid back to the railing.

"Ysabella!" I shouted, pushing myself away from the wooden barricade. In the crush, I couldn't see my friend. Brother Gille slid by me, stopping when he hit the railing, and I grabbed at his sleeve. "Brother Gille, please, find Ysabella! I don't know where she is!" The monk nodded and started to scrabble along the deck.

At that moment, the railing gave way.

Brother Gille and the others who were up against the barrier went over first, but Owen, Raymond, and I slid right after them. There was no way to stop, nothing to grip. For an instant I was airborne; then I hit someone who grunted and gave way beneath me. I sank quickly in the murky river water. Swimming was second nature to me, though. I wriggled out of my heavy kirtle and struggled upward toward the sunlight I could see glimmering above me.

I broke the surface with a gasp and immediately began to choke from the stench. Bodies floated around me. Some struggled and shouted—soldiers weighed down by armor, monks flailing in their cassocks. Some bobbed on the water like human corks, bloated and rotting. I felt a scream of horror rising, but I pushed it down, whimpering, and started swimming. I could see the shore clearly; it wasn't far. There were people standing there, waving their arms wildly.

Cries of *help!*—*au secours!*—came from every direction. One voice sounded familiar. Was it Raymond? I splashed in a circle, looking for him. What was it Ysabella had said? *I know for a fact that he can't swim.*

"Raymond!" I shouted. "Raymond!" I had lost all my French and even my English; nothing but his name came to me.

"Here!" I heard and turned again to see an arm raised high. "Help me!"

I swam toward him, trying to avoid the bodies. But it was impossible. I knocked against one, sending it spinning in the water like a maple seed twirling through the air. It was—had been—an old man. His gray hair floated like discolored seaweed. I dodged a little boy. He'd been seven or eight, perhaps. I was desperately grateful that his eyes were closed.

At last I reached Raymond. His heavy cloak was pulling him downward, and I wrenched it off and let it sink. "Lie back," I told him. "No, no, do not pull on me. You will drag us both to our deaths. Just lie back. As if you are abed."

Obediently, Raymond lay back in the water and tried to float. He was panting with terror. I looped my arm under his chin, resting his head on my shoulder. Many were the times I'd pulled a child to safety who had swum out too far for his strength. I knew what to do.

Kicking hard, I swam for the shore. There was no way to avoid the bodies. I just elbowed them aside, trying not to notice the spongy yielding of water-swollen flesh against my own skin. And then it was shallow enough for me to stand, and I pulled Raymond upright.

He bent over in the knee-deep water and retched, the river running from his lungs. Then he and I staggered to the grassy bank and collapsed, as the farmers who had been watching rushed to us.

Raymond allowed the farmers to wrap him in a musty blanket, but I shrugged off the coverings they offered and struggled back down into the water. Staring off toward the ship, which was now half-sunk and almost on its side, I saw something that made my heart leap: Owen was swimming toward me, someone clinging to his back. I waded out waist deep and reached for him as he stood. His passenger slid off, choking and whimpering.

"Help him!" Owen commanded, and I grabbed the man and raised him to standing. Water streamed off his bald head. When his eyes met mine, I gasped: It was Bishop Denis. His red hat had been lost, but he still wore his heavy scarlet robes.

"Oh, Your—Your Excellency!" I managed. "Here, let me help you. Take my arm!"

The bishop gripped my arm so tightly I was sure he would leave a bruise. He was trembling. I half led, half carried him up the slope to the spot where Raymond sat, swigging a tankard of ale that one of the farmers had provided.

"It is the bishop!" I said to Raymond.

"Leave him to me," Raymond told me. He seemed more himself. "Find Ysabella!"

I helped the bishop to sit and handed him Raymond's tankard. He took it gratefully and gulped, then coughed, spraying ale over me. I splashed back down into the river, scanning it. A dozen swimmers had reached shore by now. Others struggled in the filthy water. I couldn't bear the thought of swimming back through the press of bodies, so I did it without thinking, pushing the dead aside and grabbing the living. One soldier nearly pulled me under with his desperate fear and the weight of his armor, but I hit him as hard as I could in the face, stunning him and stopping his flailing long enough to pull him to the shallows. Over and over I went back in, towing and dragging monks and soldiers to safety. Nowhere did I see Ysabella.

Amid the frantic braying of the trapped horses, the *Saintespirit* finally sank with a great gurgle, creating a whirlpool that pulled at me. I was exhausted, but I thrashed my arms with my last strength and heaved myself toward shore. I stood in the mud and looked out over the river. There was no more movement. Only the long dead and newly drowned remained in the water.

Weeping, I stumbled up the bank and collapsed in a heap beside Owen. "She is dead," I wailed. "Ysabella is dead!"

"No, no!" Raymond protested. "No, look there. *Grâce à Dieu*, look over there!"

I blinked the blinding tears away and looked where he pointed. Down the riverbank I saw two figures staggering toward us. As they approached, I recognized Ysabella's dark hair, plastered to her face and neck. The other was Brother Gille, dressed in nothing but his linen breeches, which sagged from the weight of the river water. As he came closer, he tried to cover his naked chest with his hands.

I lurched to my feet and ran to Ysabella, throwing my arms around her.

"I thought you were drowned," I whispered. Ysabella clasped me tightly and stroked my wet hair.

"Not drowned, though nearly," she said. "Brother Gille rescued me! I panicked, and he pulled me downstream, away from the bodies."

Owen joined us, hugging Ysabella hard. "That's twice now Brother Gille has saved you," he noted. "You owe this man your life."

"I do," Ysabella said. She let go of me and went to Brother Gille, sinking down on one knee. "You have saved me from certain death two times, Brother. How can I repay you?"

Brother Gille flushed. "Oh, Mistress, no. There is nothing . . . no. I just—I didn't . . ." His color faded suddenly, and without warning he vomited at Ysabella's feet. Then he sank into a crouch, covering his face with his hands. His humiliation was complete.

Owen threw an arm around the monk. "Come along, Brother. Let's find you a tunic and something to drink." He led the monk away from Ysabella, and she joined Raymond and me. The farmers had built a fire, and we sat as close as we could, warming ourselves. The sun was going down, and the air had cooled.

Owen came back and reported, "Master Eduin— this is his farm—says we can sleep in his outbuilding, those of us who will fit inside. The other farmers have gone to find us food." To the bishop he bowed and said, "Your Excellency, Master Eduin offers you a bed in his home. The lord of the manor died two years ago, and the manor itself is deserted, not habitable. There are only the farmhouses left in Saint Veranus. It is not what you are used to—"

"It will suffice," the bishop said. Without his hat he looked quite ordinary, and he seemed to have left some of his fussy formality in the foul waters of the

Rhône. "But first I will give the Apostolic Pardon to those we have lost—in case our Holy Father's consecration of the river includes only those who died from the Sickness and not those who have drowned." On shaky legs, with Owen helping him, the bishop made his way back down the bank and stood ankle-deep in the mud. He felt for his bag, which contained the items he carried with him to perform the sacraments while traveling. But the river had swallowed it.

His high-pitched voice wavered as he began. "*Ego facultate mihi ab Apostolica Sede tributa, indulgentiam plenariam et remissionem omnium peccatorum tibi concedo et benedico te. In nomine Patris, et Filii, et Spirtus Sancti, Amen.*" By the end, he sounded more like himself.

"Amen," the survivors on shore repeated, and the prayer was finished.

The farmers brought dry clothing and what little food they had. The bishop sat and ate among us. After the meal, he sent two soldiers ahead to Avignon, to tell the pope what had happened and ask for fresh horses and provisions. Before he retired to Master Eduin's humble cottage, another farmer came up to him, kneeling before him and kissing his ring.

"Your Excellency," he said, his voice quavering with nerves. "I have the greatest of favors to ask of you."

Raymond raised an eyebrow. The rest of the group hushed.

"What is it?" Bishop Denis asked. He seemed quite recovered, though he now wore a straw hat donated by a field worker that made him look very odd. His upper part was farmer, his lower, bishop.

"Our priest has been dead this past year," the farmer said. "And my son wishes to marry. Would you— would you perform the marriage mass?"

Brother Gille and several of the others looked shocked. There were quite a few priests among the shipwreck survivors who could have done the job; to ask the bishop to perform such a ceremony for common folk was a great presumption. But Bishop Denis didn't seem to think so. It appeared that his brush with death had given him a humility that he had only pretended before.

"We owe you and your village a great debt," the bishop said. "I would be pleased to perform the mass. But we must do it tomorrow, as we will have to leave as soon as possible to return to Avignon."

"Oh, Your Excellency!" the farmer breathed. He kissed the bishop's ring again, and then urged a young couple forward. "This is my son Gervase and his betrothed, Florie. We are honored, and so grateful!"

The couple knelt and kissed the proffered ring, and the bishop smiled benevolently on them. "The sacrament of marriage is a blessing," he said. "And you will be doubly blessed, with myself performing your wedding mass."

I hid a smile. So the bishop had not achieved complete humility after all!

After an uncomfortable night on the cold, hard ground—we decided not to join those who slept in the farmer's outbuilding—Ysabella, Raymond, Owen, and I met the other survivors as we tramped down a dirt path to the tiny village that was the center of the farmers' lives. It consisted of only a few rickety wattle-and-daub cottages and barns, and a small stone church with a stone cross mounted at the front.

We gathered at the steps of the church, and Bishop Denis, looking much more well rested than anyone else, stood on the top step. He had changed his straw hat for a red hood. The bride and groom stood before him, dressed in what was obviously their best clothing, clean tunics for both and a fresh linen headdress for Florie. Ysabella went up and offered Florie her own brooch to fasten her kirtle. Though I knew the stones were only colored glass, it was clear that the bride had never seen anything so splendid.

"Keep it," Ysabella said. "It is my gift to you, for good luck." Florie protested, but Ysabella insisted, and finally the couple agreed to accept the gift. No doubt, I thought, the brooch would become their most prized possession.

The couple looked very young to me; surely Florie wasn't much older than I was. But I knew that a girl was lucky to find a living boy to marry at all these days, and far luckier to find one she liked. And it was obvious these two cared for each other. They clasped hands, blushing, their eyes downturned, as the bishop stood on the top step of the church and asked, "Do you agree to marry, and to cleave only to each other, to obey the commands of God and observe the sacraments?"

"We do," the groom said, and the bride beamed and said, "Oh yes!" The onlookers chuckled at her enthusiasm.

"May your union be blessed with good fortune and many children," the bishop intoned, making the sign of the cross over the couple.

The mass included a great deal of Latin and numerous litanies. It was clearly much longer than the masses the farmers were accustomed to; snores punctuated the bishop's prayers. But at last it ended, and the entire company—all the villagers and all the survivors from the *Saintespirit*—paraded to the biggest of the village buildings, a barn that the villagers had quickly emptied of its hooved inhabitants. A long trestle table was laid; jugs of ale and loaves of bread were scattered along its length. There were bowls of pottage and of berries. It wasn't quite a feast, but it was plentiful and good, and the happiness of the newlyweds was contagious.

"Dance! Dance!" some of the farmers called out when a fair amount of ale had been consumed. Raymond and Ysabella looked at each other.

"We could sing," Ysabella said. "To pay for our supper."

"Our instruments are at the bottom of the Rhône," Raymond noted.

Ysabella stood up from the long bench. "Does anyone have a drum?" she called. "Any other instrument?"

After a few minutes, a little boy ran up with a makeshift drum. "I have this, it's mine!" he said proudly.

"May I play it?" Owen asked him, and the boy nodded, jumping with excitement.

"We still have our voices," Ysabella pointed out, when no other instruments were produced. "They'll have to do. But—do we have to sing our sacred songs?"

"As long as we leave out the bawdy tunes, I don't think the bishop will object," Raymond said. "Let's start with 'Have All My Heart.' It is surely romantic enough for the occasion!" He hummed a note, and we began, with Owen tapping out the rhythm on the little drum.

The villagers were surprised when we started to sing, but quickly some began clapping out the beat while others rose from the table and started dancing. Their dances were a little like the ones I remembered from my own village, simple and energetic and merry. The bishop seemed not to mind the secular music; he sat at the head of the long table, smiling benevolently, his hands clasped on his round stomach.

I felt unfocused, almost dazed, as I sang. I could hardly believe we were celebrating this way, less than a day after so many had perished in the shipwreck. So near the river filled with bodies. But I had learned that was what always happened. People died, and those remaining tried to live.

Ysabella, noticing my unsteadiness, reached out and took my hand. We smiled at each other, a little shakily, and kept singing. The dancers made a big circle, holding hands, with the newlyweds in the center, and pranced around them as if they were a maypole, moving closer, then farther away, ducking under one another's arms, twirling and clapping. We performed the most rhythmic, happiest songs we knew, Owen keeping time, and for hours, as the long, late-spring twilight settled on the village and the stars poked through the blanket of the sky, the farmers—and then the soldiers and sailors—danced their joyful dance to celebrate love found in a world of loss.

They are gone, Astrid and Thyra and Tola. And their husbands, Ivar, Knud, Olaf. But oh, their weddings! They are the best part of the year, the weddings at summer solstice. The long, long days of celebration, when the sun barely dips below the edge of the sea. The joy of the brides, the pride of the bridegrooms, the plankefish *and rye bread, the mead and ale. Sometimes we would dance to the beat of a drum, more and more wildly as the festivities went on. Everyone was happy, even those who weren't entirely pleased with the partner their parents had chosen.*

Their deaths are terrible, of course. And their new babies die with them. Was there a reason for their weddings, if they leave nothing behind?

I am the only one who remembers them. Is there a reason for that?

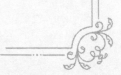

Chapter Fifteen

IT TOOK US TWO DAYS TO WALK TO AVI-
gnon. We spent the night at an abbey beside an arched
bridge that spanned the Rhône and set out early the
next morning. I sighted the high, thick walls that surrounded Avignon when we were still far from the city.
Soaring above the walls were a series of crenellated
towers—nearly a dozen in all.

"That is all the Palace of the Popes," Raymond told
me. "They have been building it for scores of years,
and it is not finished yet."

When the guards at the gate saw Bishop Denis, we
were allowed in without question. The streets were
crowded with monks and priests, noblemen and traders;

they stared at us as we passed. It seemed that word of our shipwreck had spread throughout the city.

And what a city it was! We walked past churches and chapels and a long, low building that Raymond said was a university where men did nothing but read and learn. I thought Raymond was joking when he said this, and Ysabella had to smack him to get him to stop laughing at me.

There were shops of all kinds selling meat and fish, cheese and bread, wool and silk fabric, wheels and barrels, boots and candles and arrows. Though there were some poor people on the streets, most of them appeared wealthy, in embroidered cloaks and fine leather shoes. I was no longer unnerved by the sounds and smells of cities, but I was astonished at the prosperity of Avignon.

"It is the center of all Christendom," Raymond told me. "The great wealth of the Church resides here, so people flock to take advantage of it. Once Rome held that position, but no longer."

We walked to the Palace of the Popes, next to the cathedral. It was the biggest building I had ever seen. "The biggest in the world," Raymond claimed. Part of it, on the far end, was still under construction and webbed with scaffolding.

"How many rooms does it have?" Ysabella breathed.

"Oh, hundreds," Raymond said. "And each filled with statues and paintings and tapestries. It would take you longer to see them all than it took us to walk here from Saint Veranus."

The sailors took their leave, heading into the town to find taverns to slake their thirst. The soldiers went to the stables with their horses, and we entered the massive complex with Bishop Denis and his men. Servants, alerted to our approach, waited there to take us to bedchambers. The sun had set, and we were exhausted. I lacked the energy even to look around me as we walked through the vast palace. The servants led Ysabella and me to a chamber, and we stumbled inside and onto the soft bed, too tired even to disrobe. We were asleep in minutes.

The morning light through the tall, arched windows woke me. For a moment I lay and stretched luxuriously. Then I noticed a wooden tray on a table beneath the windows, and I sprang up. Bread and cheese and cider—oh, but I was starving! I stuffed the fine-milled bread into my mouth, washing it down with cider so quickly that I nearly choked.

"Hungry, are you?" Ysabella teased from the bed. She came over to join me, and we ate every scrap of food on the tray, gazing out the window to the cloister below. Monks passed back and forth, trotting with great purpose as they went about their tasks.

I splashed my face with water from a pitcher and bowl decorated with blue and gold flowers. The objects were so lightweight and delicate that I feared they might shatter in my hand.

"So beautiful," I breathed, tracing the pattern on the bowl.

"Everything is beautiful—look around!" Ysabella said, spinning in the center of the room. The walls and ceiling were painted with hunting scenes, the floor inlaid with patterned tiles. The coverlet on the bed was silky soft and embroidered with vines holding great bunches of red grapes.

"Surely not every room is like this," I said.

"Some are far fancier," a voice said from the doorway. Owen stood there smiling. "You look much better this morning, both of you!"

"It is restful not to be in prison, or drowning," I said, and Owen laughed.

"Brother Gille has stopped by our room next door and offered to show us part of the palace. And he says the Holy Father wants to hear us perform this evening!"

"Oh my," Ysabella said. "He's told the pope himself about us?"

"Bishop Denis did. Because I—well, I saved his life, I suppose. Brother Gille says His Holiness is grateful—to us! It seems that the bishop is a favorite of his."

"How clever of you to save him, then!" Ysabella said, cuffing him on the shoulder.

We trooped through the halls of what Brother Gille said was the Old Palace, built before Pope Clement's time. The ceilings were immensely high, and every inch of every room was decorated—painted with frescoes, hung with tapestries and paintings, or embossed with gold leaf. The New Palace, still under construction, had taller ceilings yet, and still more gold. Even Raymond seemed taken aback by the opulence.

"I've seen the Grand Audience Hall and the Great Chapel before, but no more than that," he said. "I had no idea there was—all this!" He swept his arm around, indicating the immense banquet hall we were in, the Grand Tinel. Its walls were painted gold and green and red; its arched windows rose high. Long tables draped with rich cloth lined the room.

"This is where you will perform later tonight," Brother Gille said, and I drew in a quick breath. "There will be a banquet to welcome Bishop Denis back into the fold. But before that, His Holiness would like to speak with you."

"With us?" I squeaked. I couldn't imagine speaking to the pope. It was unthinkable, ridiculous. I was nobody—a fisherman's daughter. A girl without a home, with no belongings at all. I couldn't possibly talk in the presence of the pope!

"He wishes to communicate his gratitude for saving his envoy."

"But I have nothing to wear!" Ysabella cried, and Raymond let out a hoot of laughter.

"Ah yes, what does one wear to meet the pope?" he asked. "I am still picking dead minnows from the Rhône out of my breeches—I am sure they are not suitable!"

Brother Gille laughed. "We will bring you some new clothes," he promised. "It is the least we can do."

Brother Gille was as good as his word. Back in our chamber, Ysabella and I found a warm bath and new kirtles and shifts waiting for us. The shifts were of the finest linen, not the least bit scratchy, and the kirtles were real silk. Ysabella's was yellow, with green embroidery, and mine was blue, embroidered in gold. I couldn't stop stroking the smooth fabric. It was as soft as rabbits' ears. There were even shoes, supple leather that hugged our feet as if they'd been made just for us. We combed our hair with a wide-toothed ivory comb.

"Leave your hair down," Ysabella advised. "It's the same color as your embroidery. You look so pretty!"

"So do you," I said, gazing at her. The yellow gown set off Ysabella's dark curls, and her eyes flashed with pleasure as she primped before a glass that cast her own image back at her.

"Look!" she cried. "It shows both of us!"

The wavery shapes in the glass astonished me. I had never seen myself reflected in anything but water before. Was this truly me—this girl with the long golden hair, dressed in such extravagant clothes? I twirled, and the girl in the mirror twirled along with me.

"Magic," I whispered, and Ysabella laughed.

"Let's go," she said, helping me pin on my veil. She held out a hand, and I took it and clasped it tightly as we left the chamber to meet the others.

Brother Gille led us to the New Palace, where Pope Clement held his audiences. We waited in an ante-chamber with a group of painted statues at one end, life size, showing Jesus carrying his cross. Mary knelt in front of him, her arms wide, her head tilted heaven-ward. The grief on her face nearly brought tears to my eyes, and I stood looking at the statue for a long time.

Brother Gille instructed us on how to behave before the pope. "Kneel when you meet him. Kiss his ring, but do not touch his skin with your lips. Do not turn your back on him. Address him only as Your Holiness or Holy Father." I grew more anxious with every rule.

At last the Audience Hall doors opened, and we were ushered inside. The first thing I noticed was the heat. It was a warm day, but the thick walls of the palace had kept the rooms cool. Not the Audience Hall, though. It took me a minute to realize why.

Pope Clement sat on a raised dais on the papal throne, a huge marble chair decorated with a carved bull on one side and a carved lion on the other. A velvet canopy shaded the throne. On either side of the dais there was a vast fireplace, and on each of the two hearths a fire blazed. Even from the far end of the chamber, I could feel their heat. It was like standing in an oven. I couldn't imagine how the pope could bear it.

"It is to keep him safe from the Sickness," Brother Gille whispered. "His physicians advised it, to keep away the bad air. And you see, it is working! He has not been sick a day since the fires were lighted."

I had to force myself to walk forward. The pope, in his rich red velvet robes and cap, sat calmly as we approached, and his attendants stood behind him unmoving. My heart beat harder with every step. I focused on my feet in their new leather shoes. One step, then another. I could feel sweat dampening my shift. Owen's hand on my arm kept me moving.

At last we stood in front of him, below the dais. The smoke from the fires made it difficult to breathe. I forced myself to look up. The eyes that gazed back at me were deep-set, dark, but kind. A small smile played on the pope's mouth. We bowed to him, and he nodded.

"We are pleased to have you here with us," he said. His voice was low, but it reverberated in the enormous room. It was the voice of someone used to speaking to a crowd. "We have been told of your valor by our dear Bishop Denis, and how you saved his life. This is an action worthy of reward, for he is beloved by us. Which of you is responsible for this brave deed?"

Owen gulped, and Raymond pushed him forward. He walked up the two steps of the dais hesitantly. The pope held out his hand, and Owen knelt and kissed his ring.

"And you are . . . ?"

"Owen, Your Holiness. The son of a shipmaster and merchant."

"A shipmaster's son? Then it is no wonder you could perform a water rescue! But you are not French, us think—your accent betrays you."

"No, Your Holiness. I am English, from Gravesend."

"A long way from home, then," the pope said. "And what recompense do you ask for your bravery, young Owen?"

"Oh, Your Holiness, I require nothing!" Owen said. "I would have done the same for anyone. Not that the bishop was just anyone. I mean—" The sweat stood out on his forehead.

The pope chuckled. "We can see that you are the kind of man who would help a person, no matter his rank. 'Truly I tell you, whatever you did for one of the least of my brothers, you did for me.' These are the words of Jesus, and you have brought them to life. So ask what you will of us."

Owen took a deep breath, coughing a little. "I—I would like to go home. And bring Rype with me." He motioned to me. "We will go to my mother and sister in Gravesend. My father died of the Sickness, and they are alone."

The pope nodded. "Saint Timothy writes, 'But if a widow has children or grandchildren, let them first learn to show godliness to their own household and to make some return to their parents, for this is pleasing in the sight of God.' We will give you escort to Marseille, where you can find a ship to England. And you will go with our blessing." He made the sign of the cross, and Owen bowed again.

"Thank you, Your Holiness," he said. He started to turn around to descend the steps, but Brother Gille, standing with the rest of us, cleared his throat loudly. With a start Owen spun and backed down the stairs instead.

"And you!" the pope said, beckoning to Raymond. "You are a musician, we hear, and the one who guards and keeps these young ones. What would you ask?"

Raymond mounted the steps and kissed the pope's ring. He didn't seem fearful at all. "Your Holiness, this child"—he gestured at Rype—"pulled me from the Rhône, much as Owen did for the bishop. I need nothing more than my life, which I am lucky enough to have. But I do have a request . . ."

The pope raised an eyebrow. "Yes?"

"I would go to Le Puy, to live with the troubadours there. Ysabella here will come with me. But . . . my lute is at the bottom of the Rhône."

There was a moment of silence. The pontiff's lips twitched. "Are you asking us for a lute, then?"

Raymond bowed low. "I am indeed, Your Holiness."

Pope Clement tented his fingers. "Hmm. Well, we shall loan you one for your performance tonight. And if we like your music, perhaps you can keep it."

One of the pope's attendants snorted. I couldn't see Raymond's expression, but I imagined that he was smiling. "You are more than generous, Holy Father!" he said, and backed down the stairs.

"And you, Mistress," the pope said to Ysabella. She came forward, knelt, and kissed his ring. "You will go to Le Puy as well?"

"Yes, Holy Father," Ysabella said. "But I have a boon to ask of you, too."

"And what is that?"

Ysabella clasped her hands in front of her tightly. She sounded calm, but I could see how nervous she was. "My brother—my twin brother, Jacme—died of the Sickness not long ago. We had to bury him where he lay, in unconsecrated ground."

The pope leaned forward in his great throne. "Oh, my dear, all ground is consecrated for the victims of the Sickness. We have said it, and it is so."

"I know," Ysabella said softly. "But—but could you say a prayer for him? I long to know that his soul isn't suffering in Purgatory."

The pope pursed his lips. "Was he in a state of grace at his death?"

"No, Your Holiness. There was no priest there. He couldn't make his confession."

"But he was a good man?"

"Oh yes, Holy Father!" Ysabella's voice broke. "The best man I knew. He was kind to everyone, and so talented. He played the flute, and sang . . ."

"In Psalm 150, it is written, 'Praise him with trumpet sound; praise him with lute and harp! Praise him with tambourine and dance; praise him with strings and pipe!' And so your brother did. For this, we can grant him a plenary indulgence for his sins. Will that suffice?"

"Oh, Your Holiness," Ysabella breathed. She sank to her knees, and the pontiff put a hand on her head. I wasn't sure what a plenary indulgence was, but it seemed to be what Ysabella wanted.

"And you, little one—is it Rype?" The pope looked at me as Ysabella backed down the stairs. His gaze was penetrating. I breathed deeply, trying to quiet my quivering limbs, but the smoke made me cough. Slowly I climbed the stairs, knelt, kissed the ring. It was enormous, gold, intricately carved. It must have been immensely heavy and uncomfortable.

"I am called Rype, Your Holiness," I said in my halting French, "but my name is Tova."

I heard Ysabella breathe in sharply, but I didn't turn around. I got to my feet and looked straight at the pope. His dark eyes were slightly hooded, and his nose was long and hooked. He reminded me of a bird I'd seen near Essen, curious and alert, with a red head and shoulders like the pope's red cap and cape. The thought made me relax a little.

"Shall you be Tova, then? Or Rype?" the pontiff asked. He looked interested.

"Rype, I think, Your Holiness."

"And how did you come by that name? Where is your home?"

"I have no home," I said. The pope pursed his lips in understanding. He knew what I meant. "I am from the North—Norway. Everyone in my village died." I stumbled over the words.

"Are you more at ease speaking English?" Pope Clement asked. I nodded, and he said, "Then you may do so."

"I was the only one left. All my family and friends were gone." The words came to me more easily now. "Owen found me—his people said I looked like a wild bird. As you do yourself!" I stopped abruptly, horrified by what I'd said. The attendants stared at me.

"Oh," I breathed. "Oh, I am sorry. Forgive me, Holy Father! I didn't mean—"

The pope smiled, and it transformed his face. "You are not the only one who has compared me to a bird, child!" he told me. "It is the nose—like my father's, and his before him. Albert le Bec—the Beak, they called my grandfather. Ah, I have not thought of him in years!"

"They called my grandfather Finkell Fjell—*fjell*, because *his* nose was like a mountain."

The pope threw back his head and laughed, and a moment later his attendants laughed with him. I was hugely relieved.

"And how can we help you, my child?" the pope asked when the room had quieted. "Do you too want an instrument, to carry on your trip to Gravesend with Master Owen?"

I took a deep breath. "No, Your Holiness. I do not think—I do not think I want to go to England." I hadn't planned to say it; I'd had no plan at all. The words just spoke themselves. Behind me, I heard Owen make a strange sound.

"No?"

"No. I want to go to Le Puy with Raymond and Ysabella. I want to be a troubairitz."

"Do you write songs?" the pope asked.

"Yes, Your Holiness. I have written a few. I want—I want to write about my people, my family." I stopped, trying to organize my thoughts. The pope motioned me to continue.

"When I hear songs about heroes, or famous people, I can almost see them—in my mind, I mean. The songs make me feel I know them a little. But I don't want to write about warriors or kings. I want to tell about the people of my village. And—and maybe others who have been lost to the Sickness. Because . . . how else will we know that they lived?" I hoped I was being clear enough. "It seems to me that people can live on in songs. They can be remembered. I want to use my music to remember the folk I've lost. The folk we've all lost."

The pontiff nodded slowly. "'The memory of the righteous is a blessing,' the proverb says. So many have died, and we cannot remember them all. But your songs might bring them back to us, for an instant. And they may show the generations to come what we have suffered."

He understood. He understood! I turned my eyes up to his. "Yes, Your Holiness," I whispered. "That is what I want to do."

"Then you have our blessing, my child." He stood and put a hand on my head, saying a string of words in Latin that ended with "Amen."

His amen was echoed by everyone in the room. It seemed to me that it resounded off the walls and into my heart.

"Thank you, Holy Father," I said, and backed down the stairs, feeling carefully for each step so I wouldn't disgrace myself by falling on my backside.

Quickly we were ushered out of the Audience Hall after that; we had taken up far too much of the pope's time, Brother Gille informed us. He led us back through the massive corridors of the palace to our rooms to rest before our performance. I didn't dare look at Owen, and we parted without speaking.

I am very young, I think, when a group of musicians comes to our town. Five years old, maybe six. It is summertime, warm; the sun barely sinks below the horizon at night. The performers are lost, of course, or they never would have stopped. But we feed them and offer them beds for the night, and we build a bonfire in the meadow between the Haugness farm and ours. They bring out their instruments; they play and sing for us. I am breathless with watching and listening, astonished at the way everyone is transformed. Children clap their hands in rhythm, parents dance. People laugh and eat and sway in the firelight, until Father Mathias finally stops it with a scowl of disapproval and sends us off to our homes.

There was music. I had forgotten there was music.

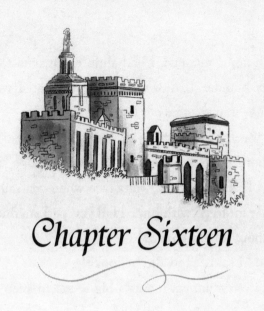

Chapter Sixteen

ALONE IN OUR ROOM, YSABELLA AND I
threw ourselves on the soft bed. "Tova!" Ysabella said.
"Your name is Tova?"

I shook my head. "Not anymore. That was another
life. I am Rype now."

Ysabella gave me an appraising look. "I like Rype
better. It suits you." Then she exclaimed, "That was
terrifying!"

"But Pope Clement was kind," I said. "And he gave
you what you wanted."

"He was wonderful," Ysabella agreed. "I would
never have thought the pope would laugh at being
told he looked like a bird!"

"Oh no," I moaned. I had almost managed to forget my blunder. "I didn't mean to say that! I was so nervous—it just came out."

"It was funny," Ysabella reassured me. "He laughed, and that's all that matters. You made the pope laugh! But—oh, did you see Owen's face when you said you didn't want to go with him? Had you said anything to him about it beforehand?"

"No," I said. "How did he look?"

"He was stunned. It was a big secret to keep from him."

I shook my head. "It wasn't a secret. I didn't even know I was going to say it until I was standing there. I had been thinking for a while that perhaps I didn't want to go to England, but I wasn't sure. And when I wrote the song for Jacme—"

"It was a beautiful song," Ysabella said softly. "And what you said to Pope Clement was right. When you sang that song, it made me see Jacme in my mind, just for an instant. The way he was when he was joyful, singing and dancing."

"That's when I had the idea of putting real people, ordinary people, in my songs. Of singing about the ones we've lost. I think I could do that in Le Puy."

"It's a fine idea," Ysabella said. "You should talk to Owen, though."

I sighed. "I know. I didn't want to hurt him."

"I think he'll understand, if you're honest with him. He's sensible. And he wants you to be happy." Ysabella patted my arm. "Have you any more of those kinds of songs—like the one you wrote for Jacme?"

"I've been working on one," I admitted.

"Teach it to me," Ysabella said. "And then we should rehearse with the others."

After a brief rest, we went to Raymond and Owen's room. Raymond sat on a cushioned bench, strumming a lute—a beautiful instrument, with inlaid wood in a floral pattern.

"Look at it!" he said. "It is the finest lute I have ever held!"

I ran my hand over the smooth finish. "It's perfect," I said. "Do you think you will get to keep it?"

Raymond laughed. "Well, of course I will! His Holiness will love our music, there's no doubt of that. And they have provided Owen with a new tabor as well."

I walked over to Owen, who stood at the window looking down at the cloister below. I put a tentative hand on his arm. He didn't turn around.

"Owen, I'm sorry," I said. There was no response. "I would have said something to you before, but I didn't know. Or I wasn't sure. I want to meet your family, truly. I love the idea of being your sister. But—but I love music more."

The words hung in the air for a few moments as Raymond strummed his lute gently. Finally Owen turned to me. "Let's take a walk," he said.

I followed him out of the room and down the hall to another of the airy, beautiful chambers of the palace. This one was deserted, though as lavishly decorated as any of the others. There was a cushioned window seat, and we walked over to it and sat.

I looked at Owen, and he tried to smile. "I understand what you said. I do. You don't know my people, you don't know England." He sighed. "But all this time I'd been imagining it—showing you my home, introducing you to Mama. She would have loved you like her own daughter."

I bit my lip. "I would have liked that. I imagined it too. It was a lovely dream—it helped me keep on when I thought I couldn't. I don't know if it is the right thing, for me to stay in France. I only know it's what my heart tells me to do."

"But I won't know what has happened to you. I

would worry—all the time. How could I find out how you fared?"

"I would worry for you too," I said, my voice unsteady. "You've done so much for me—you saved my life, over and over. Thinking of you sailing the sea—anything could happen. Storms, the Sickness . . . it would be terrible, not knowing."

Owen was quiet for a moment. Then he said, "I've had the strangest thought just now. I think I *would* know if anything bad happened to you. I feel as if there's something like a . . . a thread between you and me, and it will always link us, always pull us toward each other. Does that sound daft?"

I knew what he meant. We'd spent so much time together, seen so much of the wonders and the horrors of the world, that we were connected in a way I didn't think I could be with anyone else. "No, it's not daft at all. I feel it too. Do you think it means we will see each other again?"

"I am sure we will," Owen said vehemently. "And I know you're right, that you must listen to your heart. There's no one else to tell us what to do anymore—no parents, no elders, no priests. We have to choose our ways ourselves." He looked closely at me. "Are there other secrets you've been keeping from me, *Tova*?"

I flushed. "That one doesn't matter, does it? I am not Tova any longer. I haven't been for a long time."

"Perhaps we should all take new names to reflect how we're different," Owen suggested. "Which of us isn't entirely changed by the Sickness?" There was a moment of silence, and I thought of Jacme, dancing one of his wild dances. I could see Owen was thinking of him too.

"We should go back to the others," I said, and Owen stood up. "You aren't angry?"

"Angry? No. Disappointed, that's all." He pulled me up from the window seat. "But I do understand. There have been so many changes for you—you should be in the place that's right for you, with the people who are right for you, doing what you want to do." I had to smile then, though I felt like crying. It was the perfect thing to say.

After we'd practiced for a couple of hours, Brother Gille came to take us to the banquet. We entered the Grand Tinel and stopped at the doorway, amazed. The magnificent room, which had been empty when we visited it earlier, was now overflowing with guests. There were bishops and archbishops in their tall miters, and lords and ladies dressed in the finest silks and velvets. The tables were crowded with platters and bowls, holding foods I had never seen before—tiny roasted birds, and long, snakelike creatures in sauce; an elaborate pastry in the shape of a castle, odd-looking vegetables. Wine flowed from a fountain in the center of the room, and the plates and cutlery were gold.

"Only the Holy Father uses a knife at table," Brother Gille whispered. "He fears there may be violence if others are allowed to have them."

The monk led us to a corner with benches where Raymond and Owen could sit. We began with "*Ave Domina*," which Bishop Denis had enjoyed so much when we played it for him in Liège. The gathering quieted to listen. I could see the bishop at the pope's table, his eyes closed in pleasure.

As we progressed through our catalog of sacred music, the chatter started up again. I could see Raymond getting annoyed. It was one thing to have people talking when we played in a tavern, but he expected the highborn to listen raptly.

"Let us sing some of our ballads and rondeaux," he said at a pause in our playing, while the next course was served. "I think Pope Clement may not object."

Ysabella raised an eyebrow, but she nodded, and

we started "Sweet Gracious Face," a sad lover's song. The audience quieted. Encouraged, we went on to our favorite ballads. We played during the lengthy periods between the courses, which kept coming until I was sure everyone would burst. Every so often a servant would bring us a plate, and I tasted boar's head, roasted squab, and eels. "Disgusting!" Ysabella said, making a face, but Raymond pronounced them delicious. I thought they tasted a little like fish, but I didn't like their snaky appearance.

When the sweets had been served, and most of the company was leaning back, groaning and patting their bellies, I stepped forward. We had decided on the next song during our practice, but I was nervous.

"Your Holiness," I said, as loudly as I could. The audience quieted again, and I saw the pope look up. "Your Holiness, I have written a song—it is the kind I spoke to you about. I am sorry that it is in English, but my French is not good. I call it 'Per's Lament.' I hope you will do me the honor of hearing it."

Pope Clement nodded, indicating I should proceed. I stepped back, and Raymond struck the opening notes. He hadn't had long to learn it, but he was very quick, and he played it well. Ysabella and I began to sing.

"The dead shall rise again, I know;
Their graves remind me, row on row
Of all the loved ones who have died—
We grieve them, we who still abide.
Our happiness seems long ago.

My father fished; to sea he'd go,
Till Sickness came and laid him low.
We washed him with the tears we cried—
The dead shall rise again.

My mother felt his death a blow
From which she could not rise, and so
We lost her too, his loving bride—
The dead shall rise again.

My sister Gudrun, filled with woe,
Was next to fall to that foul foe.
In dreams she still is at my side.
The dead shall rise again.

The baby sickened; I cried, 'No!'
But Heaven turned from us below.
His last breath drawn by eventide.
The dead shall rise again.

My family lie head to toe,
Beneath the frozen earth and snow.
I pray Saint Michael is their guide.
The dead shall rise again.

It's said you reap what sins you sow,
And sorrow is the crop I hoe.
The pain consumes me from inside—
But when above them flowers grow,
The dead shall rise again."

There was silence when we were done. I didn't dare look up. They must have hated it, I thought, to be so quiet. But then a hand hit the tabletop with a loud bang, and another, and another, until I had to raise my head. The archbishops and bishops sat still, but the lords and ladies—and Bishop Denis!—were smacking the tables to show their appreciation, and some of them, men and women, had turned away to hide their grief. Pope Clement raised his hand high to me, as if giving a blessing.

"I believe they like it," Raymond said in a low voice, and I broke into a smile so wide I could feel it stretch my cheeks.

We kept playing after that, until the sun was nearly up. Every time we were ready to stop, the diners called for more. We went through our entire repertoire and had to repeat some of the songs. I sang until I was hoarse. It was glorious. I could see my happiness reflected on the others' faces, and I promised myself I would remember this moment, this flash of joy in the long, arduous journey.

In the morning, we left Avignon. We had a papal escort, a dozen armed men, and two priests to safeguard us on the trip. And Brother Gille had asked to go with us and stay in Le Puy as our spiritual advisor. I suppose the pope felt we could use a good deal of spiritual advice; he released Brother Gille from his service and gave him a papal blessing. I hoped the temptation of having Ysabella constantly nearby wouldn't be too much for him, but I was pleased he was coming. His writing was so much better than any of ours; he could transcribe all our songs in his beautiful script.

Owen had tried to persuade us to go straight north to Le Puy, but we couldn't bring ourselves to leave him before we had to. Even Ysabella, who longed for Le Puy the most, wanted to finish the journey together. It was a two-day walk south to Marseille, and we would have a papal escort, comfortable tents, and good food on the way.

Owen and I walked together most of the time. Sometimes we were quiet, and I knew he was wondering what he would find at home. Would Gravesend be a town of death like so many we'd passed, with only a few starving survivors? Or would it be one of the lucky places, nearly untouched by the Sickness? Were his mother and sister still among the living? When I noticed him sunk in such thoughts, there wasn't much I could do but try to distract him, with songs or stories or memories.

"Remember the old couple near Emden?" I asked. "The fisherman and his wife? I wonder how they fare."

"I'm sure they survived," Owen said. "We were probably the only strangers they'd seen in a year. Who would bring the Sickness to them?" I smiled, recalling their kindness, the way they'd insisted we eat their meager food and tried to get us to sleep in their bed.

"And the abbess," I recalled. "That dreadful woman!" But memories of her reminded me of Jacme, and his terrible fight with Raymond. With a sidelong look at Ysabella, I stopped talking.

"We have had some adventures," Owen acknowledged.

"More than enough to last me a lifetime," I said. "But not you, I suppose. You still want to go awandering, to sail from one end of the world to the other, don't you?"

"For a while, maybe," he said. "But one day I'll be too old to sail. I'll hand over my ships to my son, and then—"

"Your ships—your son?" I interrupted him with a laugh. "So you'll be a great merchant with a flock of ships, a beautiful wife, a fine son to take on the business?"

"A fleet of ships," he corrected me, laughing himself. "And of course, I will have those things. Do you doubt me?"

He took my hand in his rough hand, and we swung them between us as we walked. I shook my head. "I don't doubt you at all, Owen. If there ever was someone who will do what he says he will, it's you." That pleased him immensely.

When we reached the port of Marseille at last, we walked about for a time in wonder. It had a huge harbor, clogged with ships—all the vessels that hadn't been permitted to land in the northern cities seemed to have congregated there. There was barely room for a dinghy to maneuver among them. Owen was thrilled, pointing out cogs and keels and hulks, describing their differences, showing us square-rigged and lateen-rigged sails. I hadn't realized before how much he loved ships, nor how much he knew about them.

As his excitement grew, I felt more and more bereft, but I was determined not to show it. He could tell, though, as so often he'd known what I was feeling when I barely even knew it myself. That night—our last night—he sat beside me at supper at the Sanglier Inn, where we would sleep before he departed in the morning.

"You don't need to be sad," he said, as I pushed the innards of my meat pie around on my plate. "We will see each other again."

He had said that before we left Avignon, I remembered. But now words burst out of me, despite my best intentions. "How do you know?" I cried. "The seas, the Sickness, life itself—it's all peril, all a threat. Death lurks everywhere, you know that!"

Ysabella turned, disturbed at the tone of my voice. For a moment, I felt like the Rype of early days, the girl who huddled speechless in the corner, tugging on her braid to feel safe.

"We all know that," Owen acknowledged gently.

"But chance is everywhere too, and good fortune, and well-made plans. And I have a well-made plan to come back to you."

I wiped my eyes with my sleeve. "Do you?"

"Of course I do. When I have gotten too old to sail forth on business, I'll go one last time to Marseille, and ride north to Le Puy. And I'll live out my declining years with all of you, playing the tabor with a grizzled fist until I'm too deaf to hear the beat."

Raymond, eavesdropping beside us, let out his whoop of a laugh at that and slapped Owen on the back so hard he nearly fell off his bench. "We'll hold you to it, lad!" he cried. "We'll save a place for you at table and expect you in a few decades."

I loved the image that summoned up, all of us aged and bent, Raymond too old to stand, Ysabella wrinkled, her dark hair streaked with white, but as beautiful as ever, still singing, still playing, in a place that was all sunlight and contentment. I knew it was no more real than my imaginings of life in Gravesend as Owen's sister, but I held it close nonetheless.

Our farewell, in the gray light that came before dawn, was painful. Owen hugged us, each in turn, saving me for last.

"We will see each other again," he repeated to me, as I clung to him. He said it over and over, until I very nearly believed it and was able to let him go. As the sun rose, we watched him clamber into a dinghy that two men rowed out to a cog, the *Constance*. He climbed up the rope ladder, vaulted over the side, and, with one small wave of the hand, was gone from sight.

We turned away. Raymond slung one arm around my shoulder and one around Ysabella's. Brother Gille walked beside us, his lips moving in a prayer for Owen's safe travels. I didn't weep. I was sad, to be sure, but I had been so much sadder. I would miss Owen, but I didn't have to mourn him. He was alive, and he was heading home. And I was alive, and I too was heading home. As Owen had said, I was with the people who were right for me, doing what I wanted to do.

It was enough. It was everything.

"Tova! Supper!" Mama's lilting voice comes to me through the cold dusk. It is nearly the time when the sun stops rising and we live in the darkness for weeks. I bring in the last armful of wood, glad for the warmth of the hearth in our little cottage. I shake the snow off my cloak and hang it on a peg.

The table is ready, pottage ladled into wooden bowls. Per bangs a spoon on the table and tries to say my name, but it just comes out as "Ma-ma-ma." That is all he says so far. Gudrun kisses him on the top of his head and passes me the bread as I take my seat. My hands are freezing, and Papa chafes them before he picks up his own spoon. The firelight casts dancing shadows on the walls, and Mama hums a tune as she brings a bowl to Mormor in her seat by the hearth.

Papa says the blessing, and we eat. I look around the table. I am warm, and the food is good. Everyone I love is here, or nearby, or sheltered in my heart.

It is enough. It is everything.

After

Her name was Tova.

It was the name her family gave her, but they were all gone. There was no one left to call her that.

Now she was Rype, and she remembered everything.

The trip across the British Sea had been grueling. Everyone was sick except Rype. She'd had to tend to them all—Raymond, Ysabella, and Rogier, the local boy from Le Puy who'd taken Owen's place at the tabor. It reminded her at times of her weeks aboard the *Saint Nicholas*, nursing the dying sailors. But whenever those memories threatened, she told herself that nobody ever died from seasickness. They may have wanted to, but they would survive.

When they arrived at the Gravesend harbor, it was so filled with ships that their vessel had to jostle for a place. It was strange to hear English again, after five years of speaking and hearing almost nothing but French. And strange to be in a crowded town, after the tranquility of Le Puy's isolated mountaintop, and the silence of the desolate villages they'd passed through on their way to the French coast. So many of them were still abandoned, years after the Sickness. Their cottages had fallen to ruin; the forest had reclaimed their crops. Sometimes Rype thought that the world would never fully recover.

They had three nights booked at the Bell and Candle Inn before traveling on to London. The inn was run by a friend of Raymond's whom he'd known since his time in England, so many years before. It was a fancier place than most Rype had performed in, its tables unstained, its floor strewn with fresh rushes. They ate supper before they played, and Rype spent the entire time looking around, searching for a familiar face.

She had written to Owen months before, as soon as they knew their plans, but for a letter to make the trip safely from Le Puy to Gravesend—well, that was as unlikely as seeing a bear walking upright through the streets of Paris. She'd sent the note with a group of pilgrims heading from Le Puy to Santiago de Compostela, in the hope that it would find its way over the sea from northern Spain to England. She didn't really expect it would arrive at all, much less that it would reach Gravesend before they did. And she didn't really expect to see Owen. Even Ysabella had cautioned her, saying, "It was a dangerous journey home for him from Marseille, with the Sickness still raging. I don't want to distress you, Rype, but . . ."

"I know," Rype said. "It's unlikely. I can hope, though, can't I?"

"One can always hope!" Ysabella said, smiling. But her eyes were sad.

The innkeeper, Edmund, was a large, jolly fellow. He and Raymond drank vast quantities of ale, laughing and slapping each other on the back. "Did you see the flags I put up?" Edmund asked Raymond at one point. "'Come one, come all!' they say. 'Three nights at the Bell and Candle: The Wild Birds!' I planted them all over the town."

They had given their ensemble that name—or rather, Raymond had given it to them, and the others had agreed. It helped make them known, to have a name that was short and easy and memorable.

"But can any of the townspeople read?" Raymond asked, raising an eyebrow.

Edmund chuckled. "Not many! But they'll see the flags and know that something special is happening here. That's enough to bring them in."

Ysabella and Rype had fine new kirtles for the trip, and Raymond too wore new clothes, his tunic and cloak sumptuous and elegant. Rogier had combed his hair at last and looked almost presentable. The inn was full, thanks to Edmund's notices, and their performance that night was met with cheers and table thumping.

The second night, they played some of their newer pieces along with the crowd favorites. Rype had written a song in memory of Sigrid, her dear friend who was burned as a witch. It was as dark a lyric as she'd ever penned, and the listeners were silent as she and Ysabella sang.

"Do they hate it?" Rype whispered to Raymond, when no one clapped at the end.

"Indeed not," he said. "Look at their faces."

She could look straight at the people in the audience now. She wasn't afraid anymore. And Raymond was right. The horror of what had happened to Sigrid was reflected in their expressions. Tears stood in some of the men's eyes, and the few women there were weeping openly. She was grateful. Sigrid's dreadful end deserved that tribute.

And then her gaze settled on a face in the crowd, blue eyes below a shock of red hair, a joyous gap-toothed smile. Her heart leaped. It hardly seemed possible, but there he was—Owen, with a short new beard, looking like a younger version of his father. He sat between a dark-haired woman and a girl with red curls peeking out from her veil.

His mother, his sister. Both of them alive.

Rype couldn't help herself; she ran forward as he stood, and he hugged her, squeezing so tightly she could barely breathe. Stronger arms now, broader shoulders, but Owen nonetheless. Her Owen.

"You got my letter!" she cried when she could speak.

He shook his head. "No, I got no letter. But I saw the notices that the innkeeper put out. When I read the name—The Wild Birds—I knew it had to be you. Who else would have that name? Oh, my friend, it has been so long!"

"It has," Rype said. "But you look just the same. Still a skinny, wide-eyed lad."

He laughed and countered, "And you are still a gangly, speechless bird-girl!"

She was not, and he was not. But that lad and girl were still inside them.

"Owen," came a soft voice from behind Rype. She turned.

"My mother," Owen said, motioning to the older woman. "Mama, this is Rype."

"My dear," the woman said. She took Rype's hand and looked up at her for a long time. Her face was worn and lined, but she had Owen's bright eyes. "Thank you for helping to bring my son back to me."

"No!" Rype protested. "It was he who brought me to safety. I did nothing! I nearly got him killed a half dozen times!"

"You gave him a reason to keep going," Owen's mother said. Her tone allowed for no argument.

"And this is my sister Alice." Alice was about twelve or thirteen, the age Rype had been when she met Owen. She jumped up and, as Owen had done, threw her arms around Rype.

"I am so very glad to meet you!" she cried. "Owen still talks about you when he's home. It's Rype this and Rype that, and did I tell you about Rype and the rescue in the Rhône, and Rype is such a wonderful songwriter, and Rype insulted the pope himself. And now here you are!"

Even in the dim light of the inn, Rype could see Owen flush, and she laughed. "Here I am," she agreed. "And I have heard nearly as much about you!" Alice smiled Owen's gap-toothed smile and wriggled with pleasure at the thought that she had been the subject of conversation.

"Owen, are you a merchant, then? A sailor?"

"I am a master now," he said with some pride. "The *Saint Nicholas* made it back long before I did. Barnaby—do you remember Barnaby?"

"Of course," Rype said, wincing. She would never forget Barnaby's cold stare, his anger and threats.

"He died, so the others held the ship for me, hoping for my return. And since the Sickness has gone, I've made several trips, but not to France. Too perilous, still, with never knowing if the war is off or on."

Rype nodded. "You look very much the successful shipmaster."

"And you, very much the—the beautiful troubairitz."

She laughed again at his stammering. It was almost as if the old Owen stood in front of her, not a grown man with his own ship, his own business. "Thank you, sir," she said, dropping into a curtsy. "But you remind me, I must finish performing. We'll talk more later."

"Much more," Owen said. He reached for her hand and lifted it to his lips, and Rype stood stock-still for a moment before he released her. She could feel her cheeks heating, and she looked down at the floor. But she couldn't help the smile that spread across her face, and when she raised her head, she saw Ysabella wink at her.

As she went back to the group, Raymond struck a chord on his lute, the introduction to their newest song. Rype fixed her eyes on Owen's as she sang the words she'd written during the chilly winter nights in the stone house on the hilltop of Le Puy. As with most of her songs, it helped to keep the ones she loved clear and close. It went on for dozens of stanzas, but it was the first two she most wanted Owen to hear. She sang them straight to him.

"There was a maiden, lost and all alone;
Pursued by Death, she hid upon a strand—
A sailor-lad espied her in a tree,
He fed her, calmed her, offered her his hand.

They shared no language, but his eyes were kind;
She followed him into the ocean foam.
And as their ship took flight away from shore
Her heart beat like a wild bird flying home."

BACKGROUND

THE BUBONIC PLAGUE, OR BLACK DEATH, came to Europe on a ship from Asia that docked in Sicily in 1347. Caused by *Yersinia pestis*, a bacterium that was carried by fleas, it spread quickly through what is now Italy and nearly all of Europe in the next year.

The plague killed fast. It caused chills and fever, weakness, and painful swelling of lymph nodes. As it progressed, patients bled from mouth and nose and under their skin, causing black bruises to appear. Death came in a week or less.

The bubonic plague changed as it moved through the continent. In some places it became pneumonic, a form that was transmitted through the air and attacked the lungs. Few survived this form. In septicemic plague, the bacteria entered the blood. Victims nearly always died.

Nobody knew how the disease was spread or how to stop it. Some believed it was the result of bad air or bad smells, others that the movement of planets was to blame, still others that religious offenses caused the outbreak. Some blamed Jewish people for the disease. Others said that witches caused it. Doctors knew nothing about germs. They treated sufferers with bleeding, herbal remedies, and potions made from items such as eggshells, clay, precious metals, urine, and snakeskin. Of course, none of these cures helped.

Historians and scientists are uncertain of the total death toll in Europe, but they estimate that at least twenty-five million and up to fifty million people died—between 40 and 60 percent of the entire continent's population. By 1351, the disease had nearly disappeared, though it would recur often over the next centuries.

A ship from England carried the plague to Norway, arriving in 1349 with all crew members dead. Curious dockworkers ventured onto the ship and brought the fleas, or the rats that harbored the fleas, back to their homes. The town of Tusededal was so hard hit that all its inhabitants perished—all but one, a young girl. According to historian Philip Ziegler, the girl was discovered years later living like a wild creature and was called Rype, or Wild Bird. She is the inspiration for this story.

> *I call all and everyone to this dance:*
> *pope, emperor, and all creatures*
> *poor, rich, big, or small.*
> *Step forward, mourning won't help now!*
> *Remember though at all times to bring good deeds*
> > *with you*
> *And to repent your sins*
> *For you must dance to my pipe.*
>
> —Bernt Notke, 1400s

ACKNOWLEDGMENTS

I AM GRATEFUL TO SO MANY PEOPLE FOR making this book happen, but especially to:

Emily Feinberg, who wasn't scared off by the nasty stuff

Jennifer Laughran, who shepherded the story through all its incarnations

Shani Soloff, who tosses ideas at me faster than I can catch them

Debra and Arnie Cardillo, whose audio talents are beyond measure

Ben Sicker, who is always super positive

Terje Leiren, Kari Gissler, Nick Adams, Laurie Nussdorfer, and Kries Versluys, who helped me out with my (nonexistent) medieval Norwegian and Dutch

My copy editor, Linda Minton, who double-checked (and corrected) every last detail

And often last but never least, Phil Sicker, who uncomplainingly reads every word I write and then cooks me a fabulous dinner.